D1095723

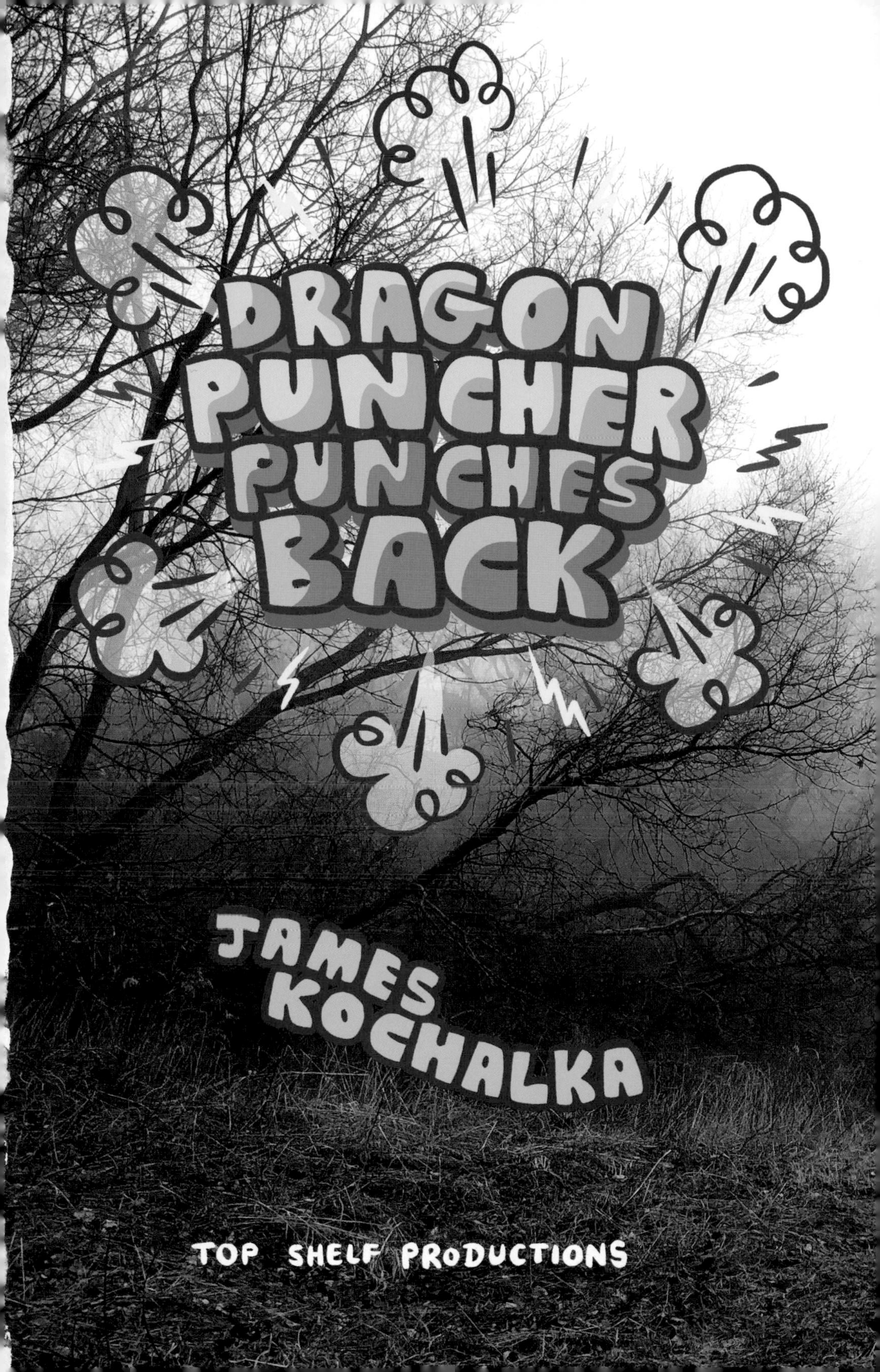
DRAGON PUNCHER PUNCHES BACK
JAMES KOCHALKA
TOP SHELF PRODUCTIONS

STARRING:

SPANDY

ELI & OLIVER

Dragon Puncher Punches Back © 2022 James Kochalka.

Published by Top Shelf Productions, an imprint of IDW Publishing, a division of Idea and Design Works, LLC. Offices: Top Shelf Productions, c/o Idea & Design Works, LLC, 2765 Truxtun Road, San Diego, CA 92106. Top Shelf Productions®, the Top Shelf logo, Idea and Design Works®, and the IDW logo are registered trademarks of Idea and Design Works, LLC. All Rights Reserved. With the exception of small excerpts of artwork used for review purposes, none of the contents of this publication may be reprinted without the permission of IDW Publishing.

IDW Publishing does not read or accept unsolicited submissions of ideas, stories, or artwork.

Editor-in-Chief: Chris Staros

Edited by Leigh Walton.

Visit our online catalog at www.topshelfcomix.com.

Printed in China.

ISBN 978-1-60309-514-3

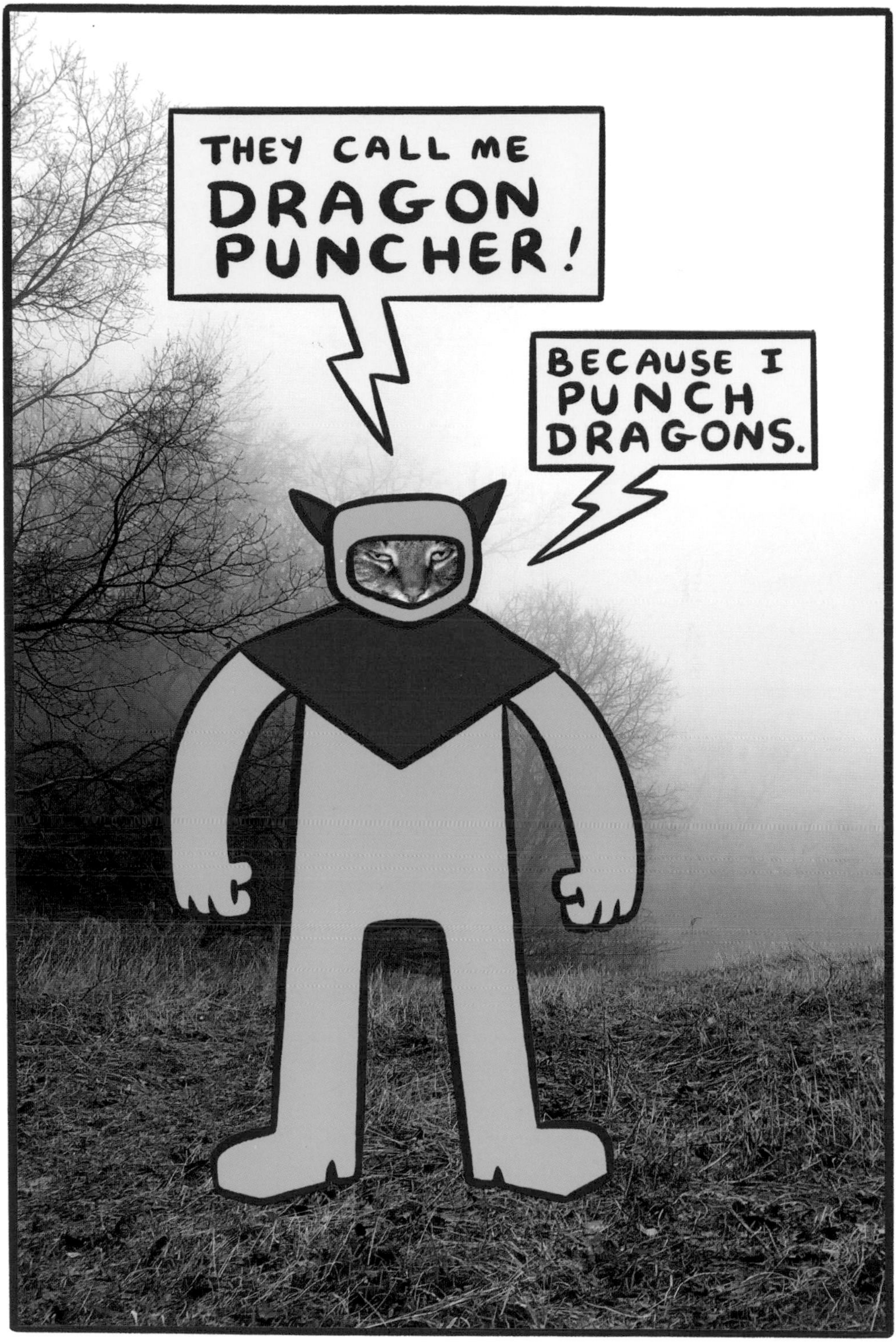
THEY CALL ME DRAGON PUNCHER!
BECAUSE I PUNCH DRAGONS.

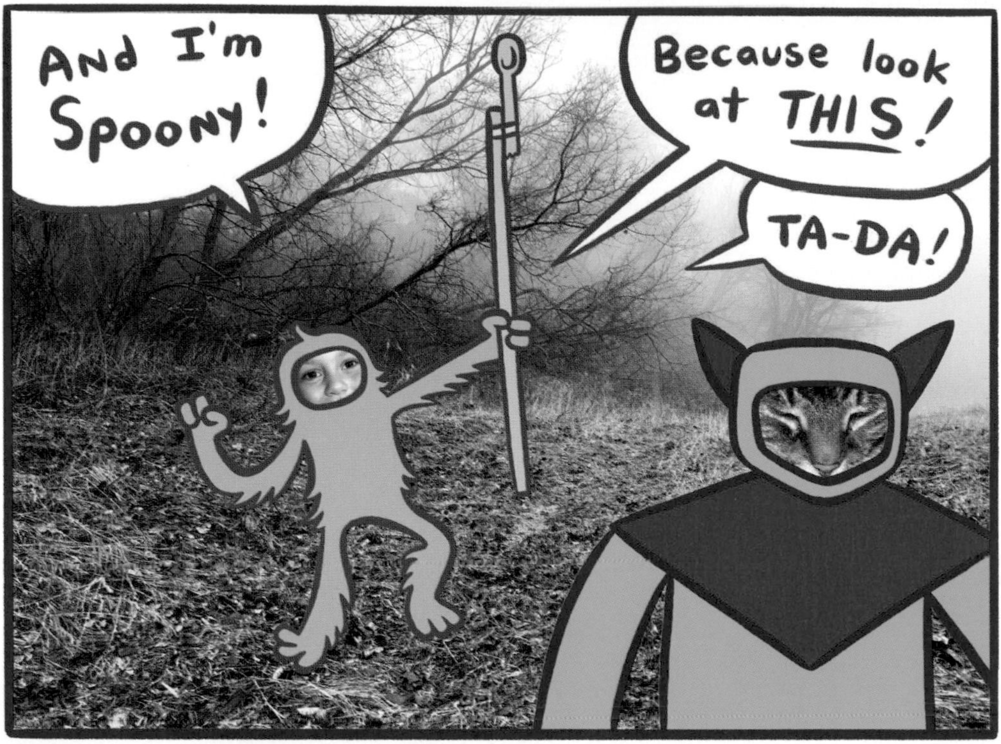
And I'm Spoony!
Because look at THIS!
TA-DA!

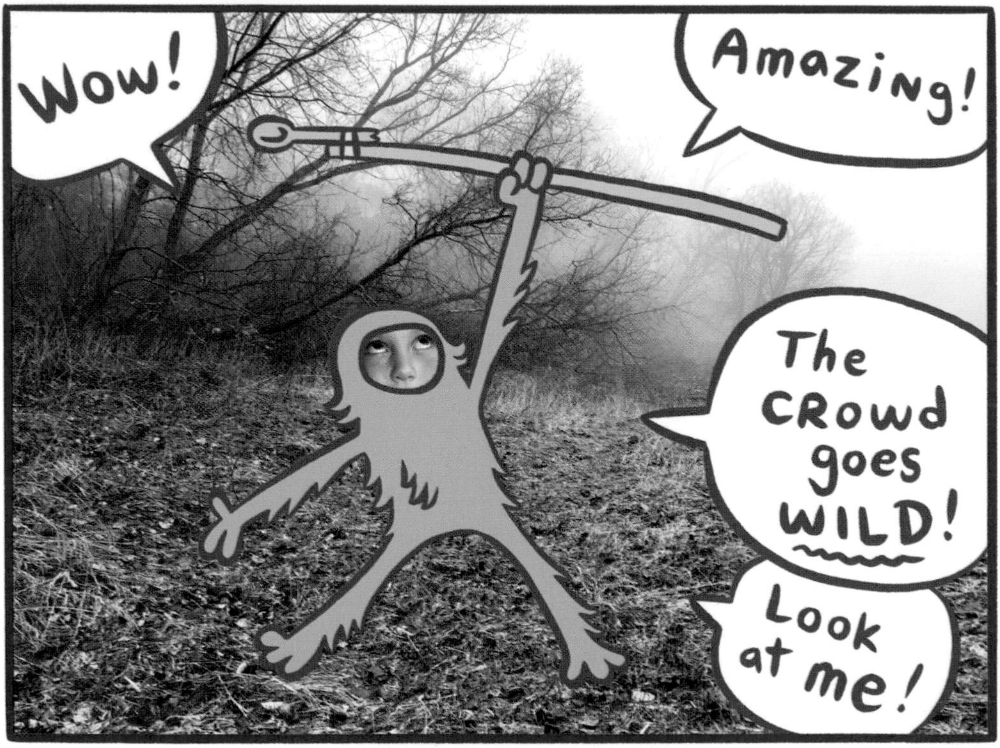
Wow!
Amazing!
The CROWD goes WILD!
Look at me!

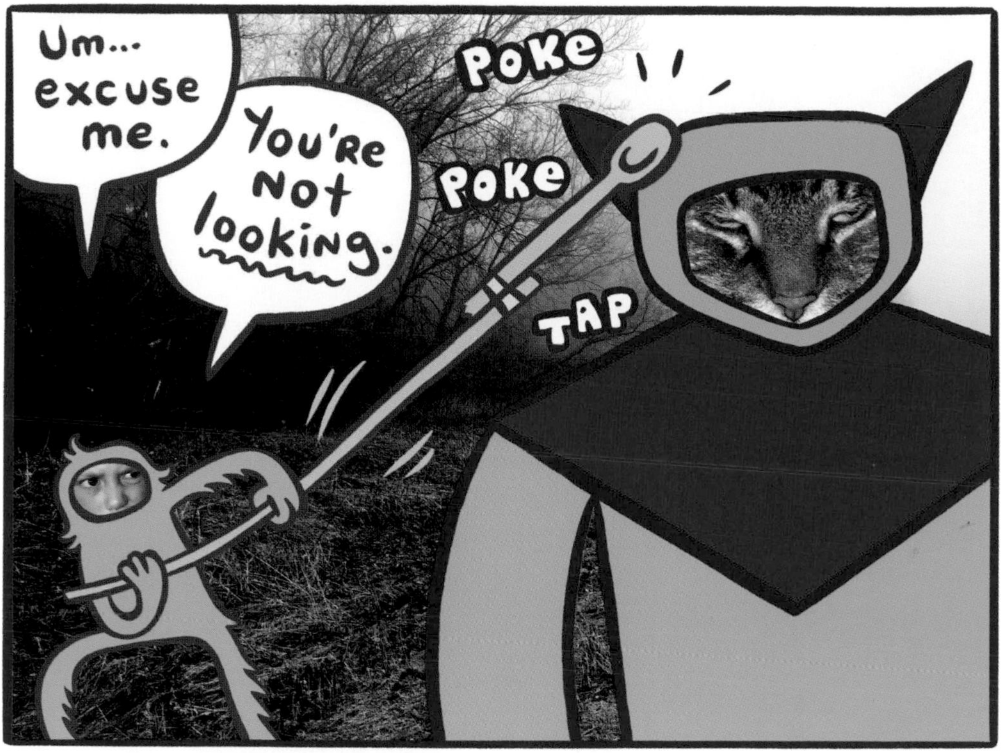
Um... excuse me.
You're not looking.
POKE
POKE
TAP

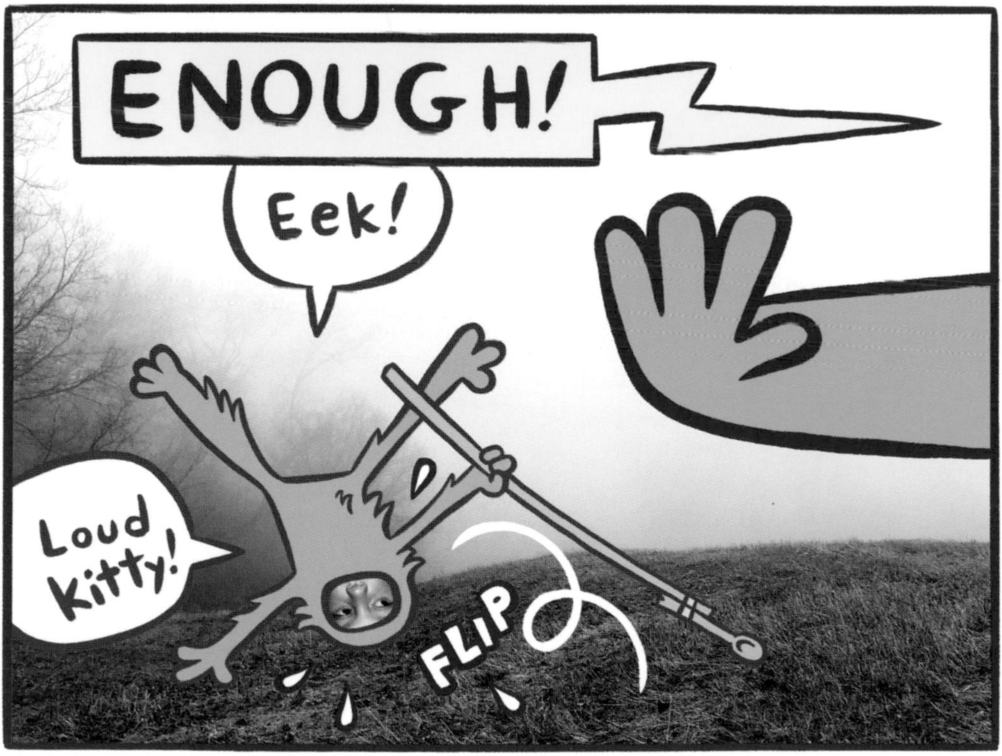
ENOUGH!
Eek!
Loud kitty!
FLIP

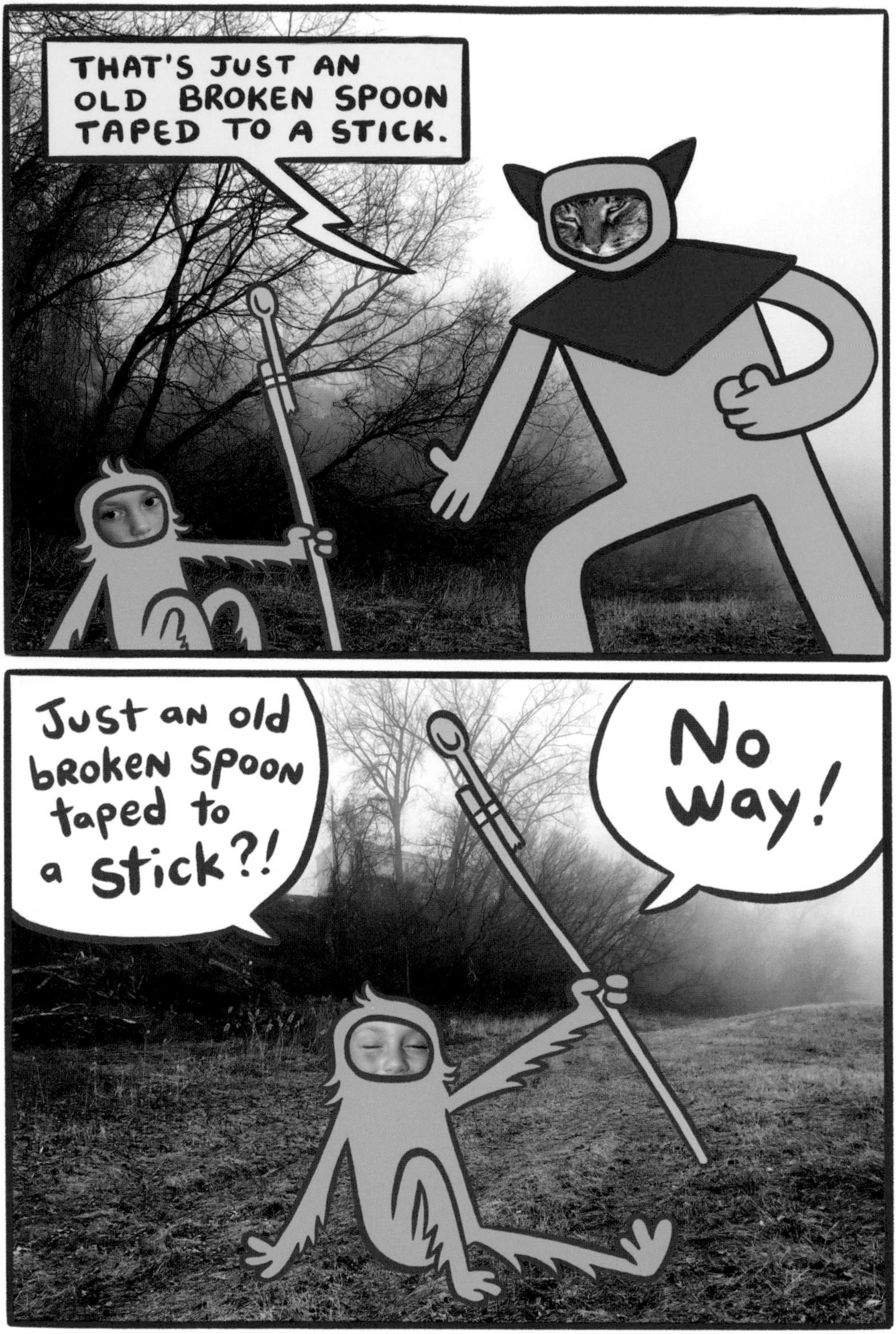
THAT'S JUST AN OLD BROKEN SPOON TAPED TO A STICK.
Just an old broken spoon taped to a stick?!
No way!

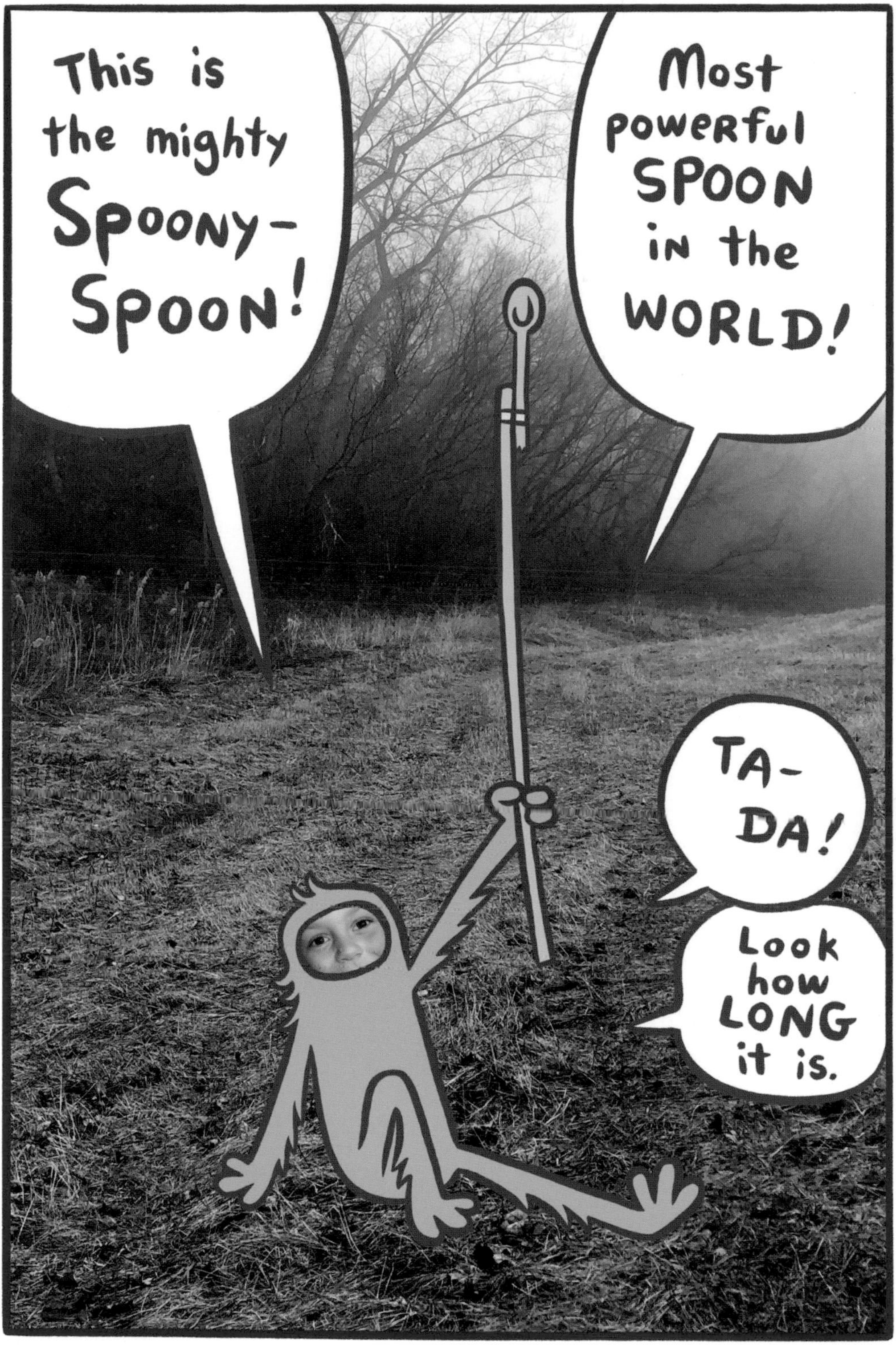
This is the mighty Spoony-Spoon!
Most powerful SPOON in the WORLD!
TA-DA!
Look how LONG it is.

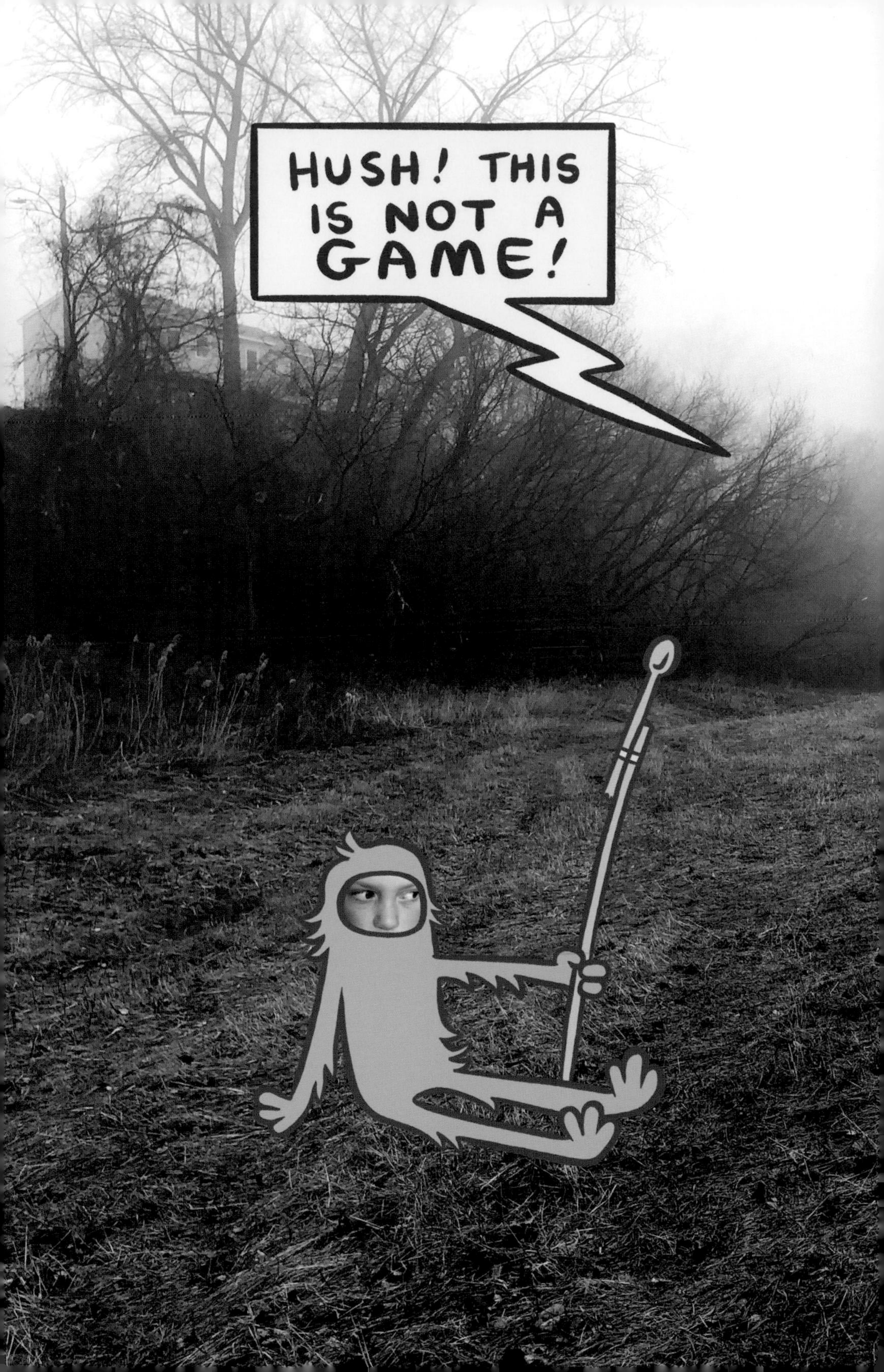
HUSH! THIS IS NOT A GAME!

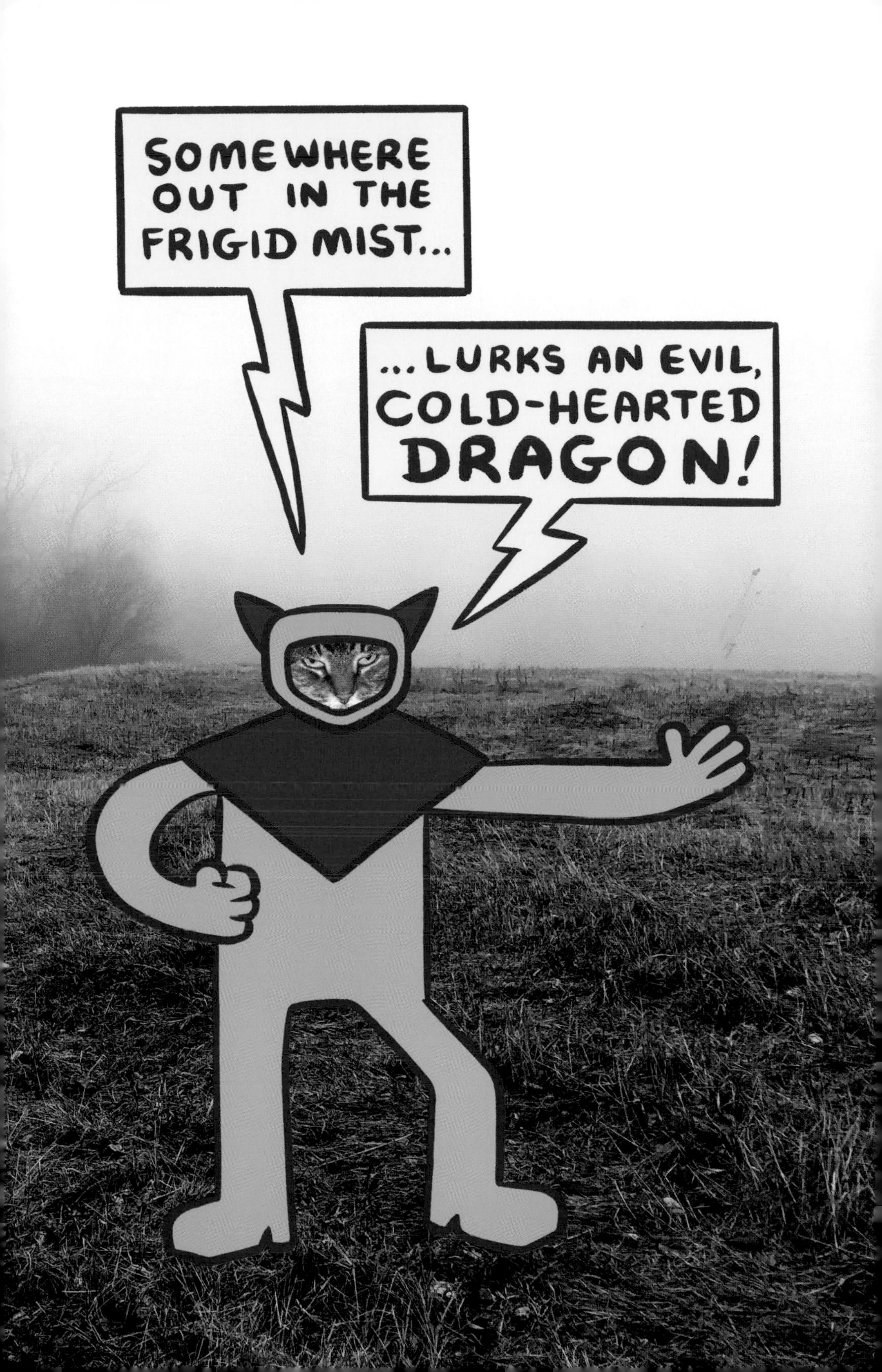
SOMEWHERE OUT IN THE FRIGID MIST...
...LURKS AN EVIL, COLD-HEARTED DRAGON!

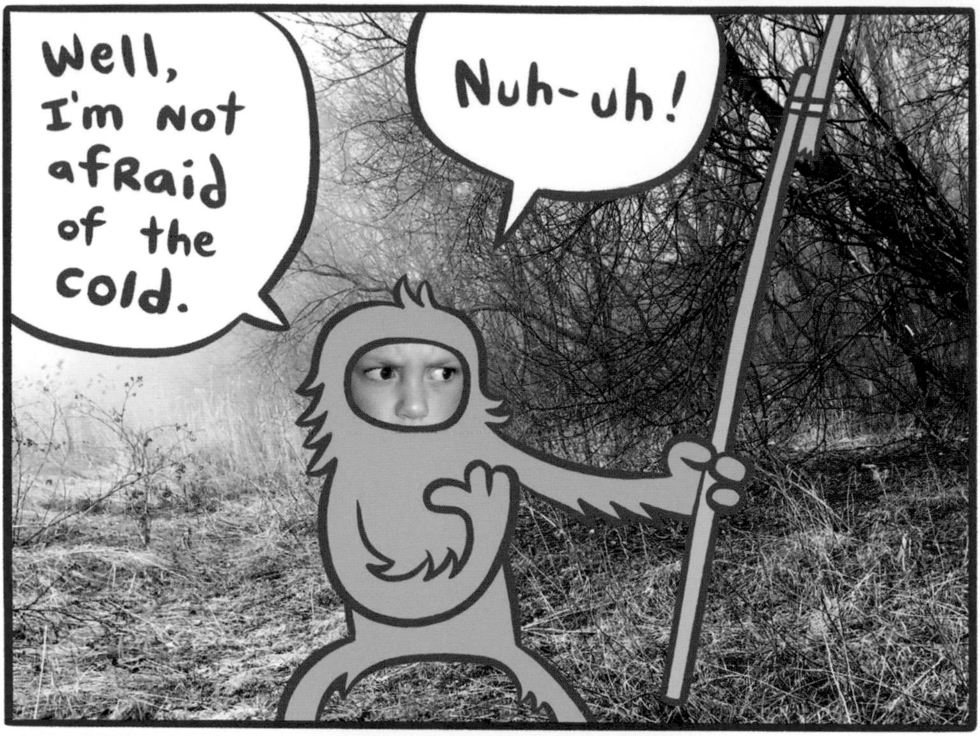
Well, I'm not afraid of the cold.
Nuh-uh!

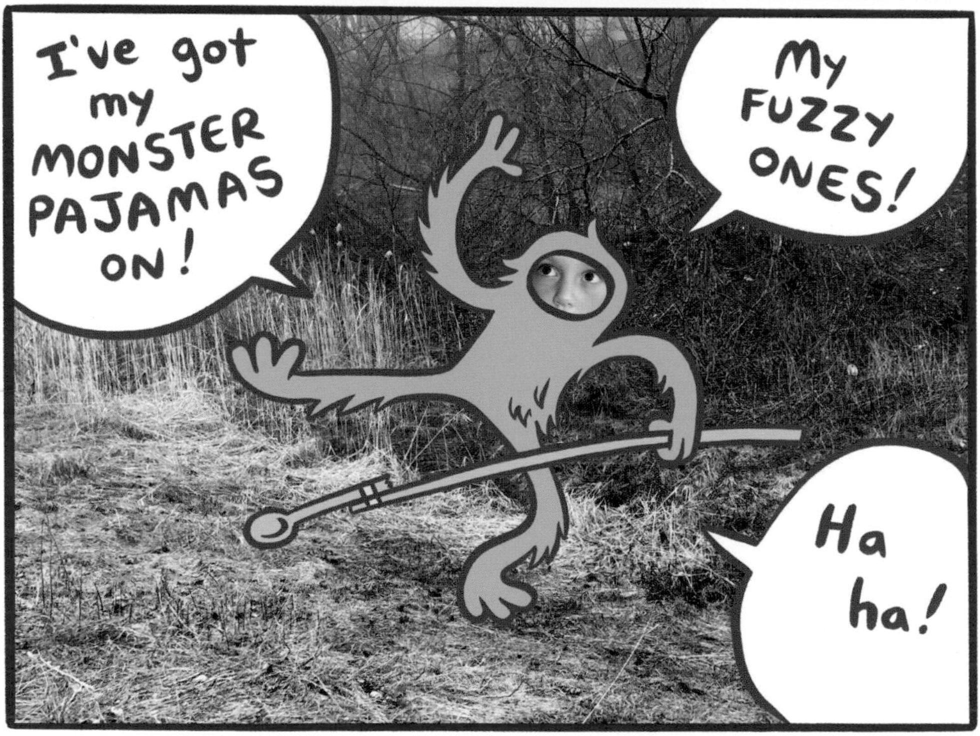
I've got my MONSTER PAJAMAS ON!
My FUZZY ONES!
Ha ha!

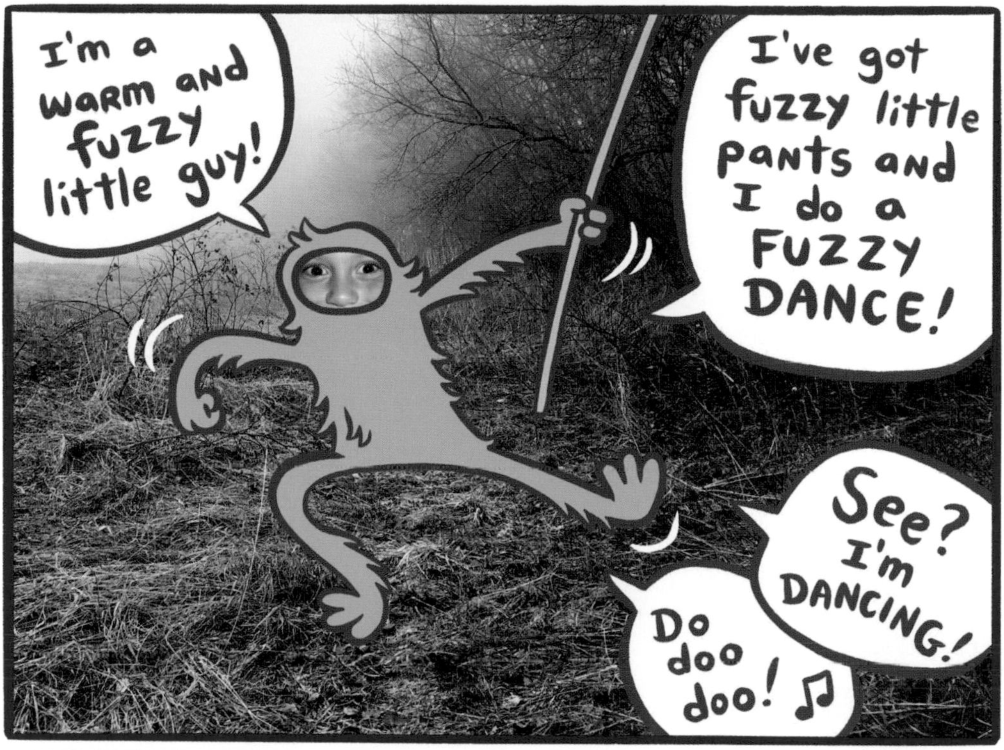
I'm a warm and fuzzy little guy!
I've got fuzzy little pants and I do a FUZZY DANCE!
See? I'm DANCING!
Do doo doo! ♫

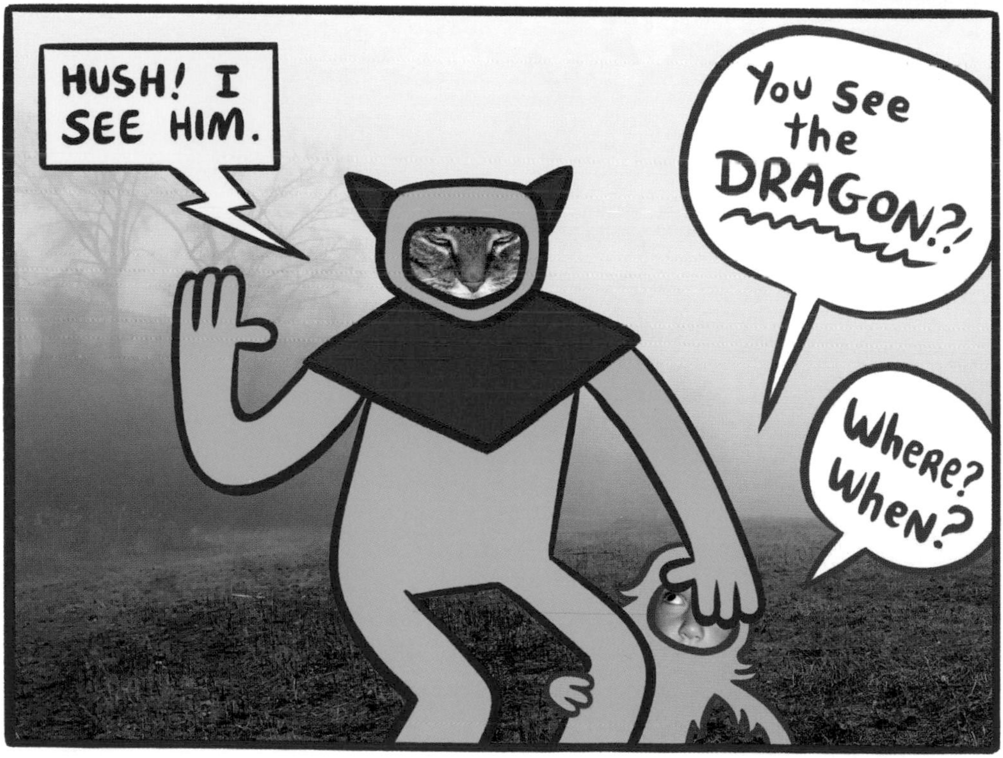
HUSH! I SEE HIM.
You see the DRAGON?!
Where? When?

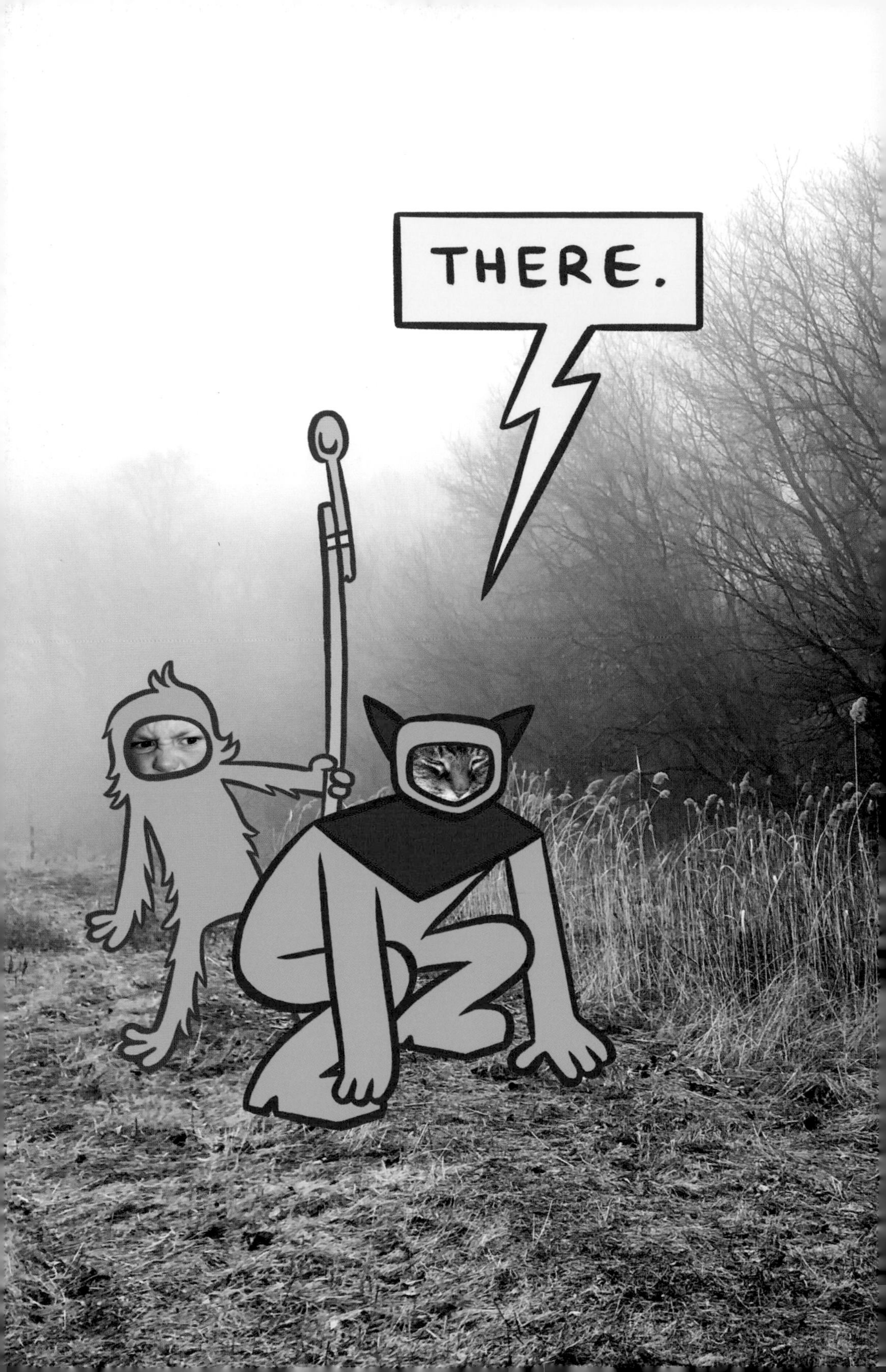
THERE.

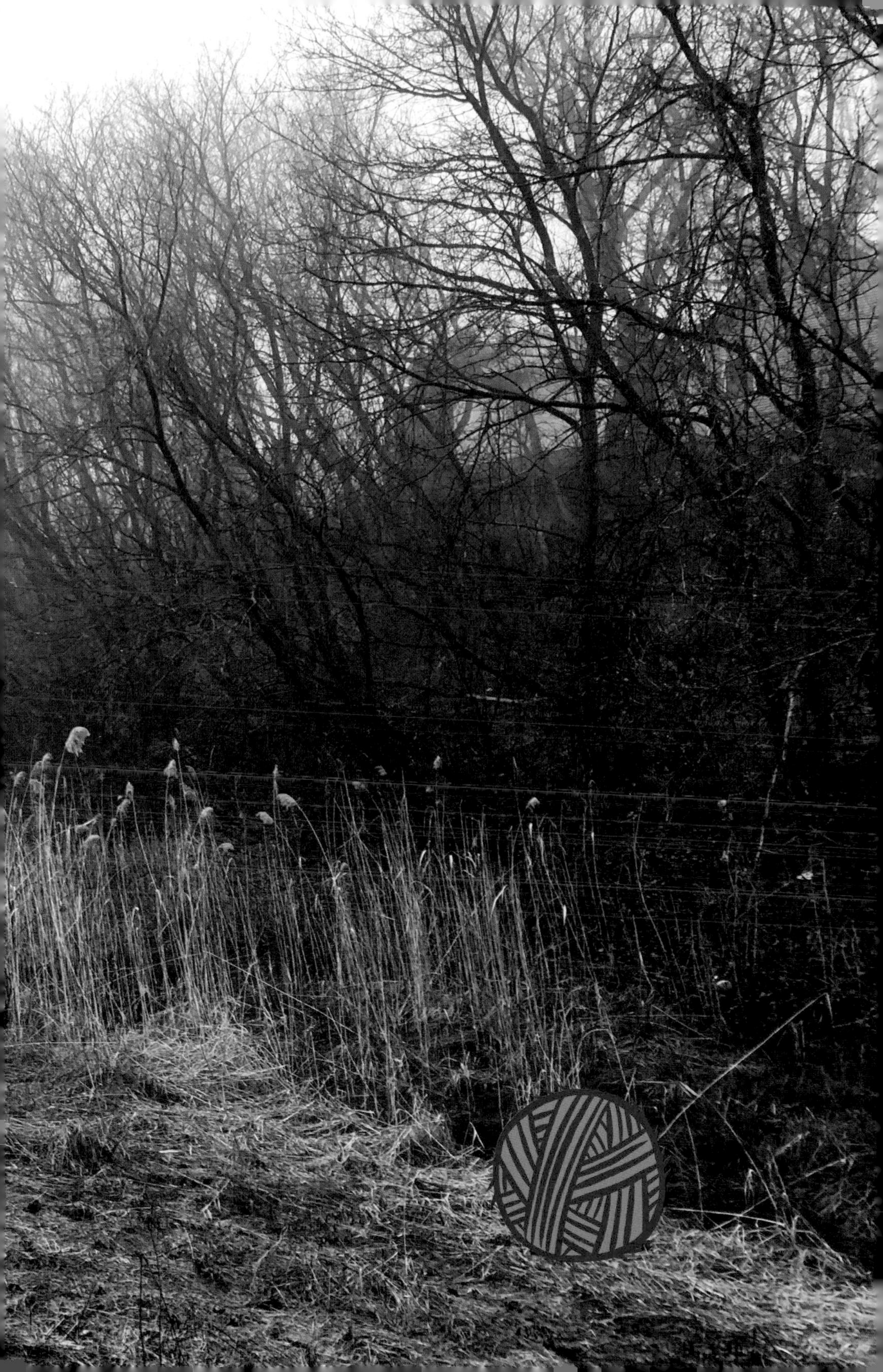

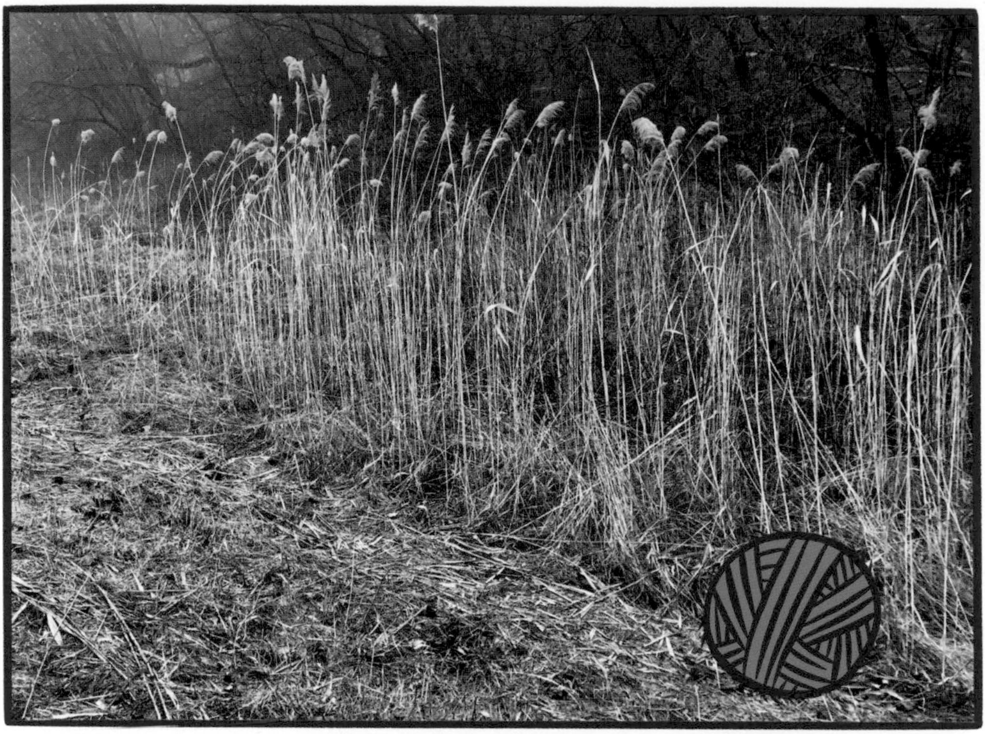

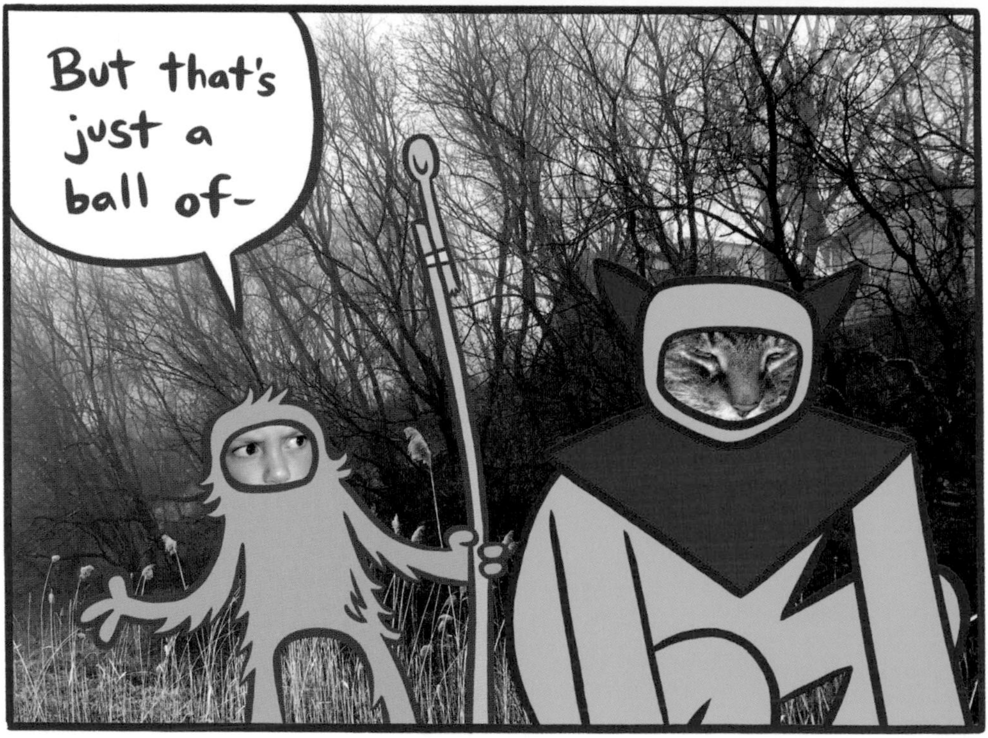
But that's just a ball of-

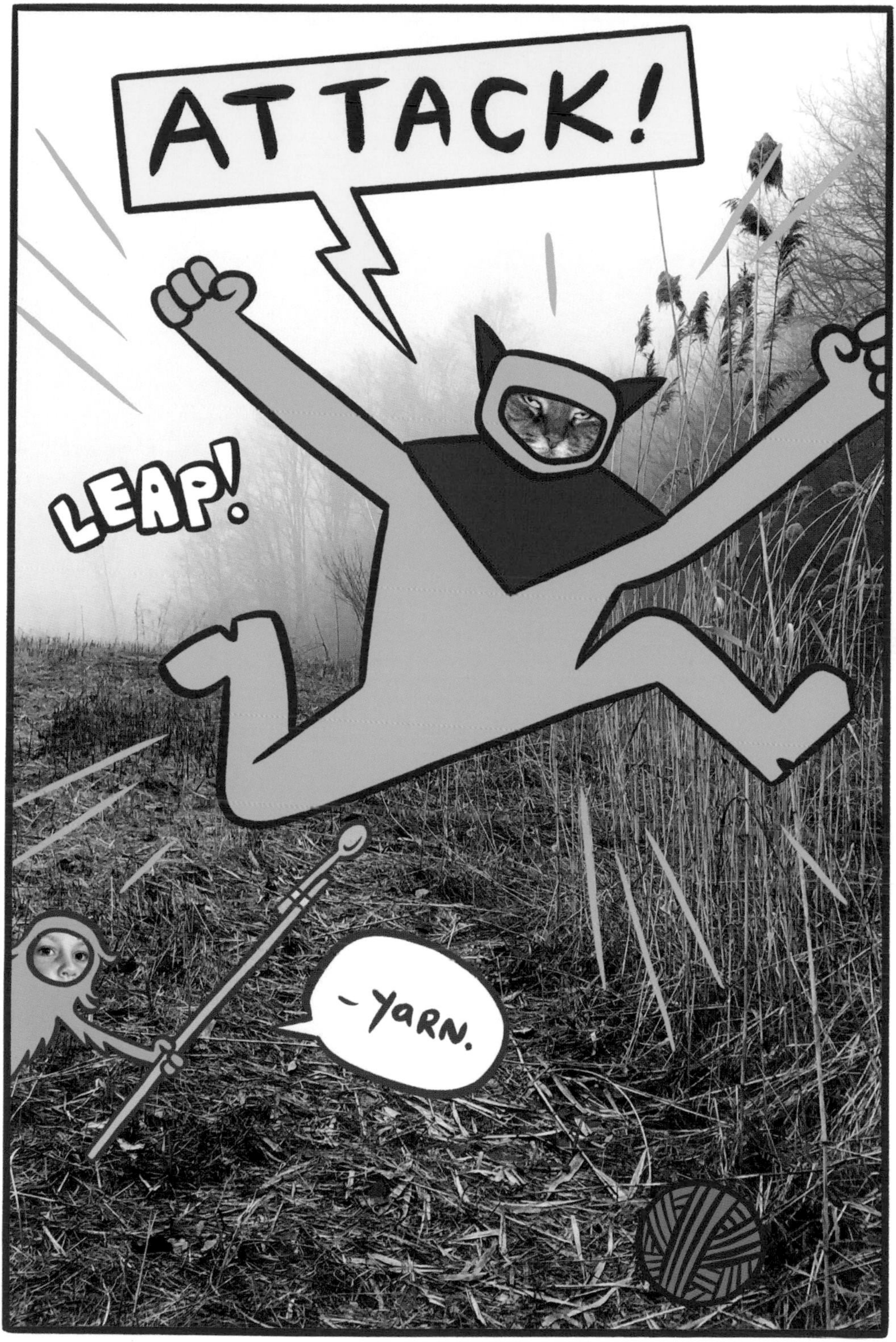
ATTACK!
LEAP!
-yarn.

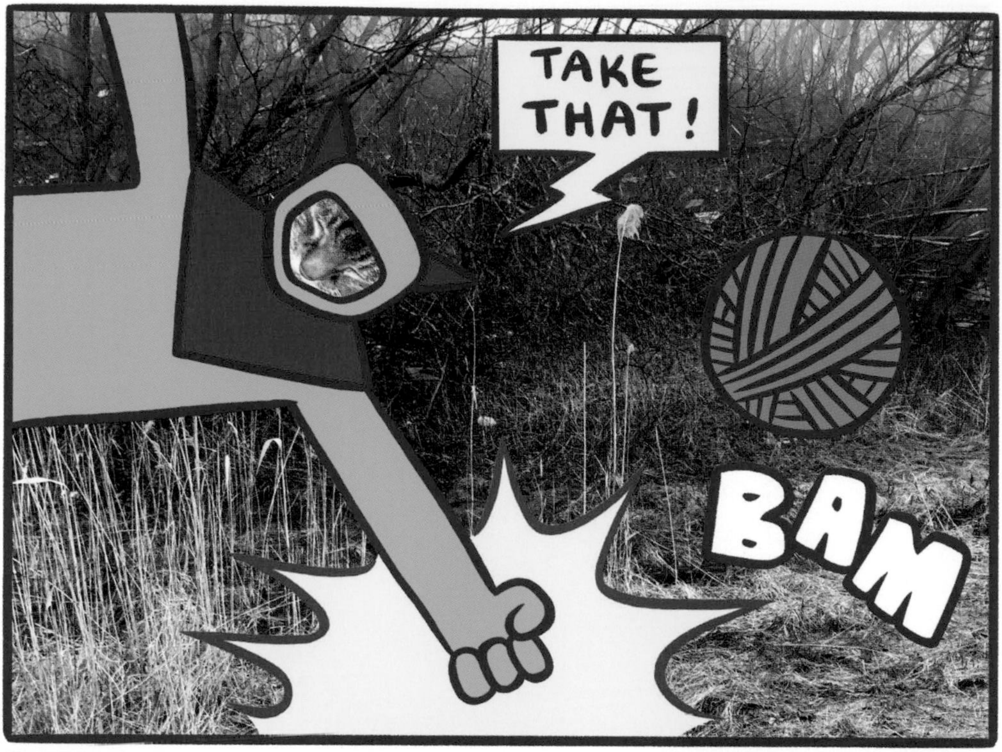
TAKE THAT!
BAM

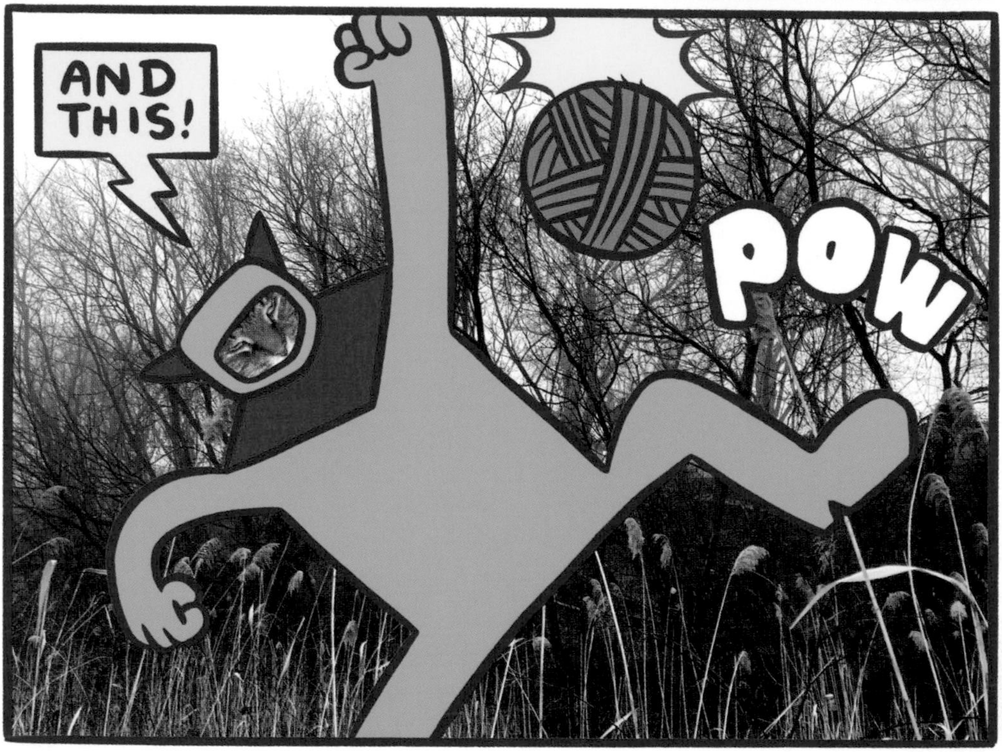
AND THIS!
POW

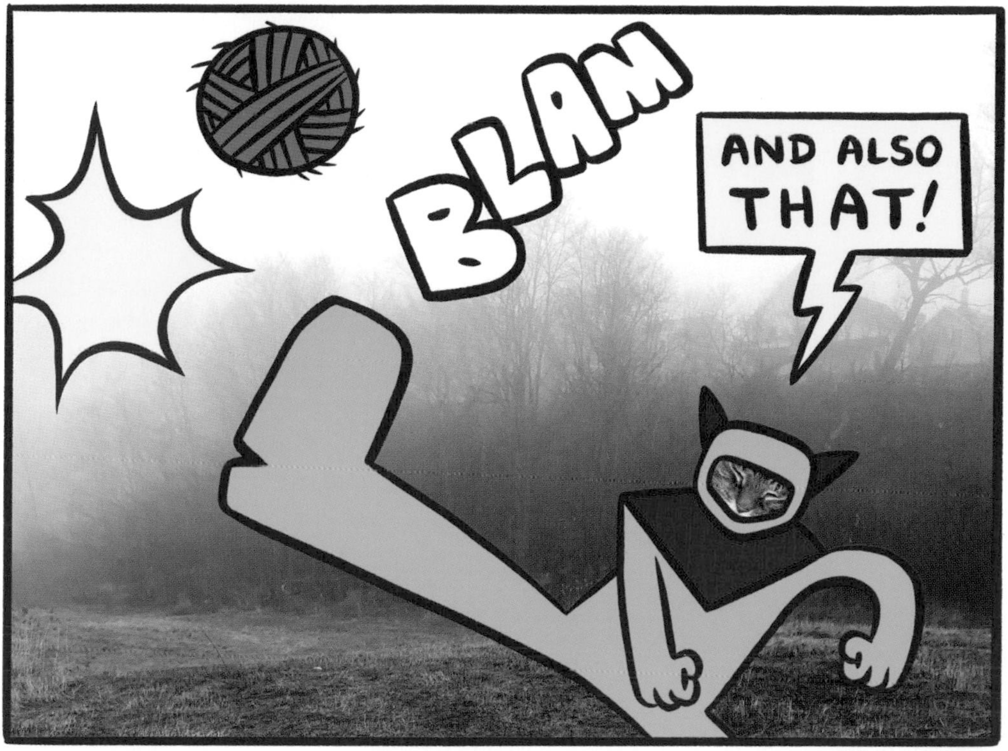
BLAM
AND ALSO THAT!

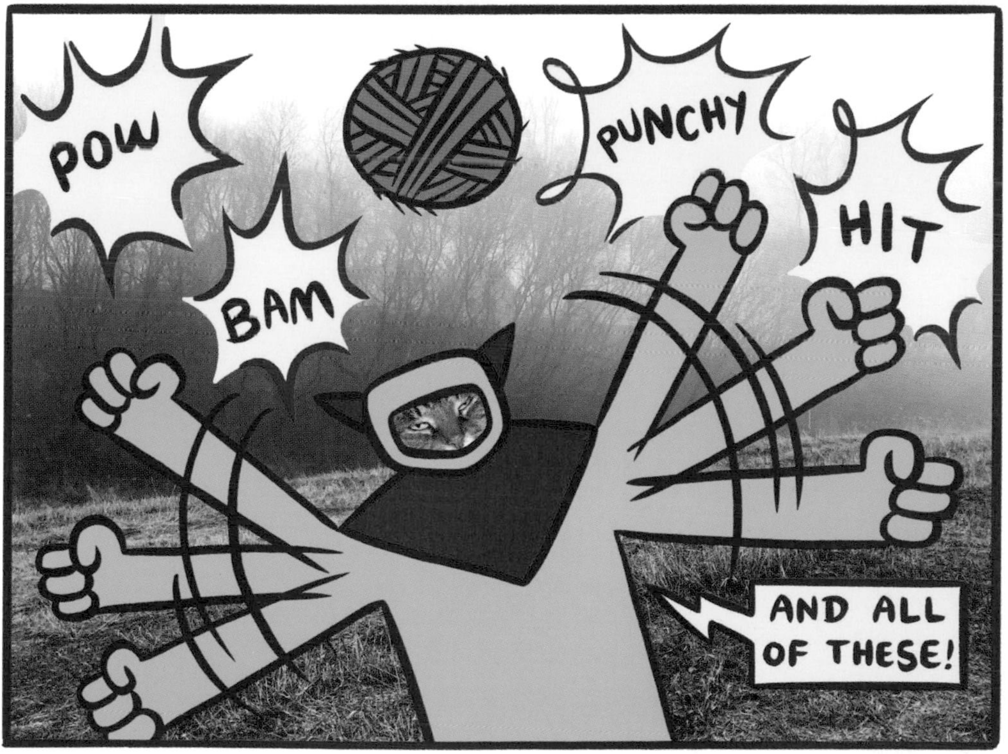
POW
BAM
PUNCHY
HIT
AND ALL OF THESE!

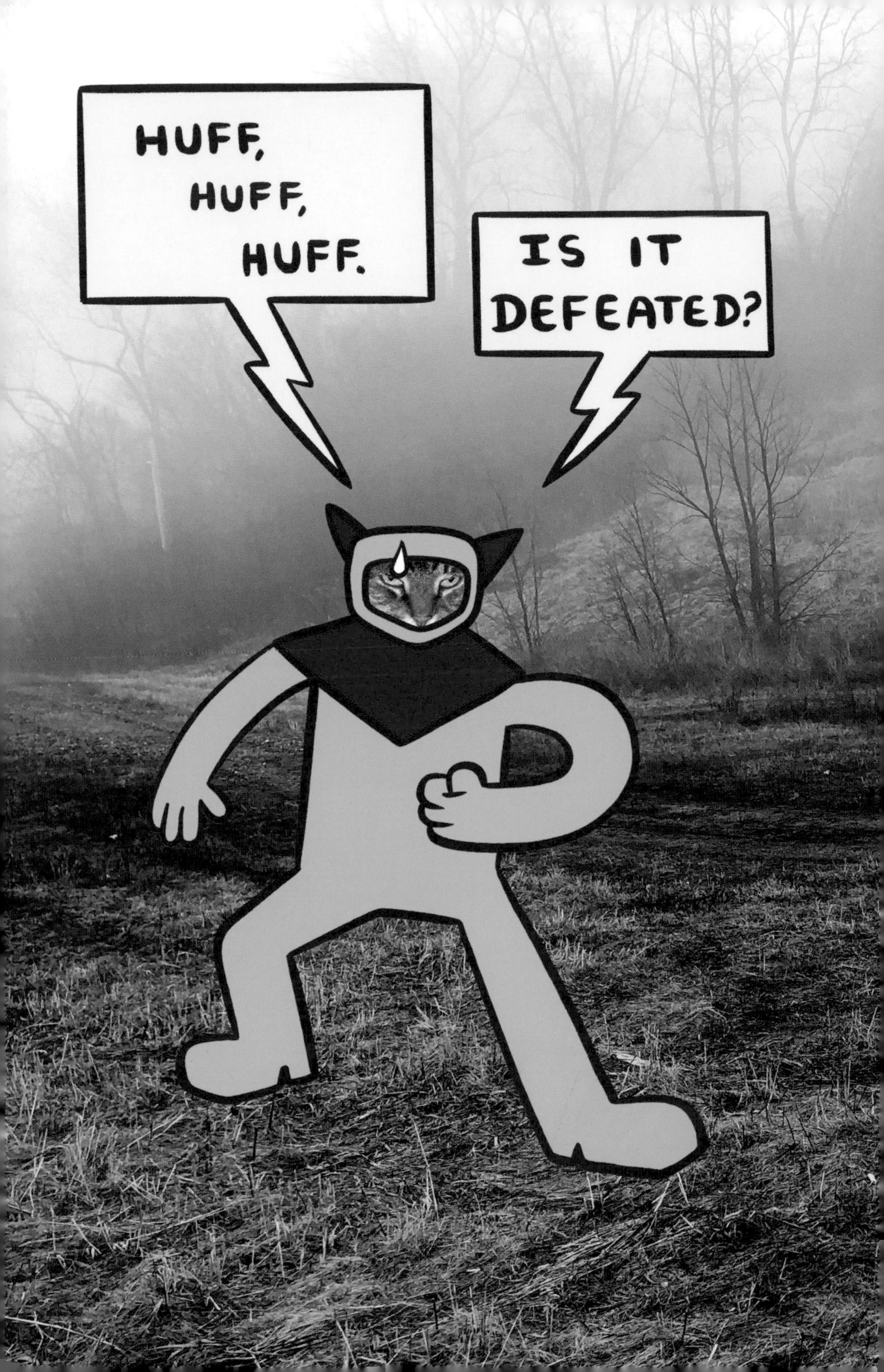
HUFF, HUFF, HUFF.
IS IT DEFEATED?

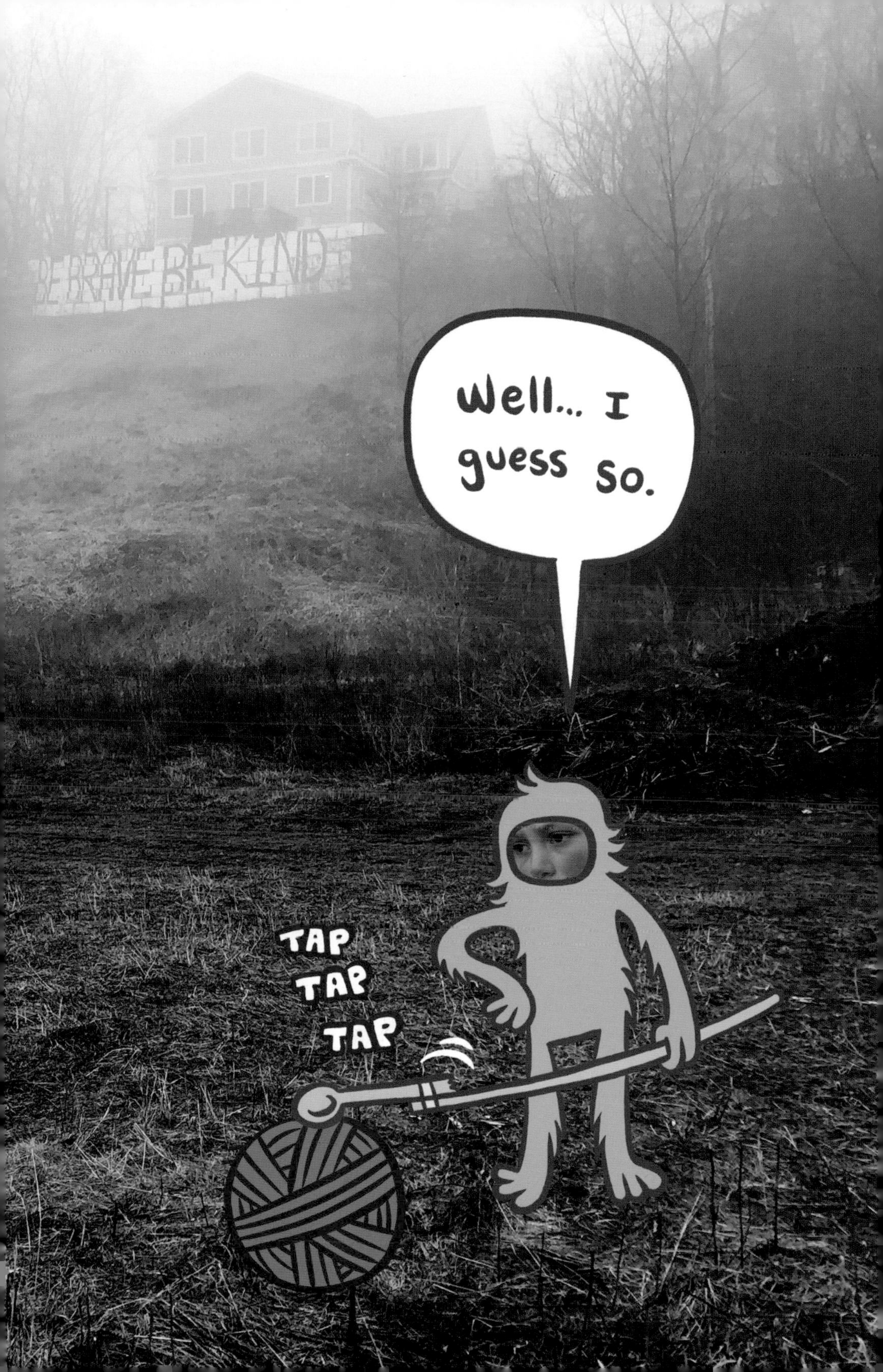
BE BRAVE BE KIND
Well... I guess so.
TAP
TAP
TAP

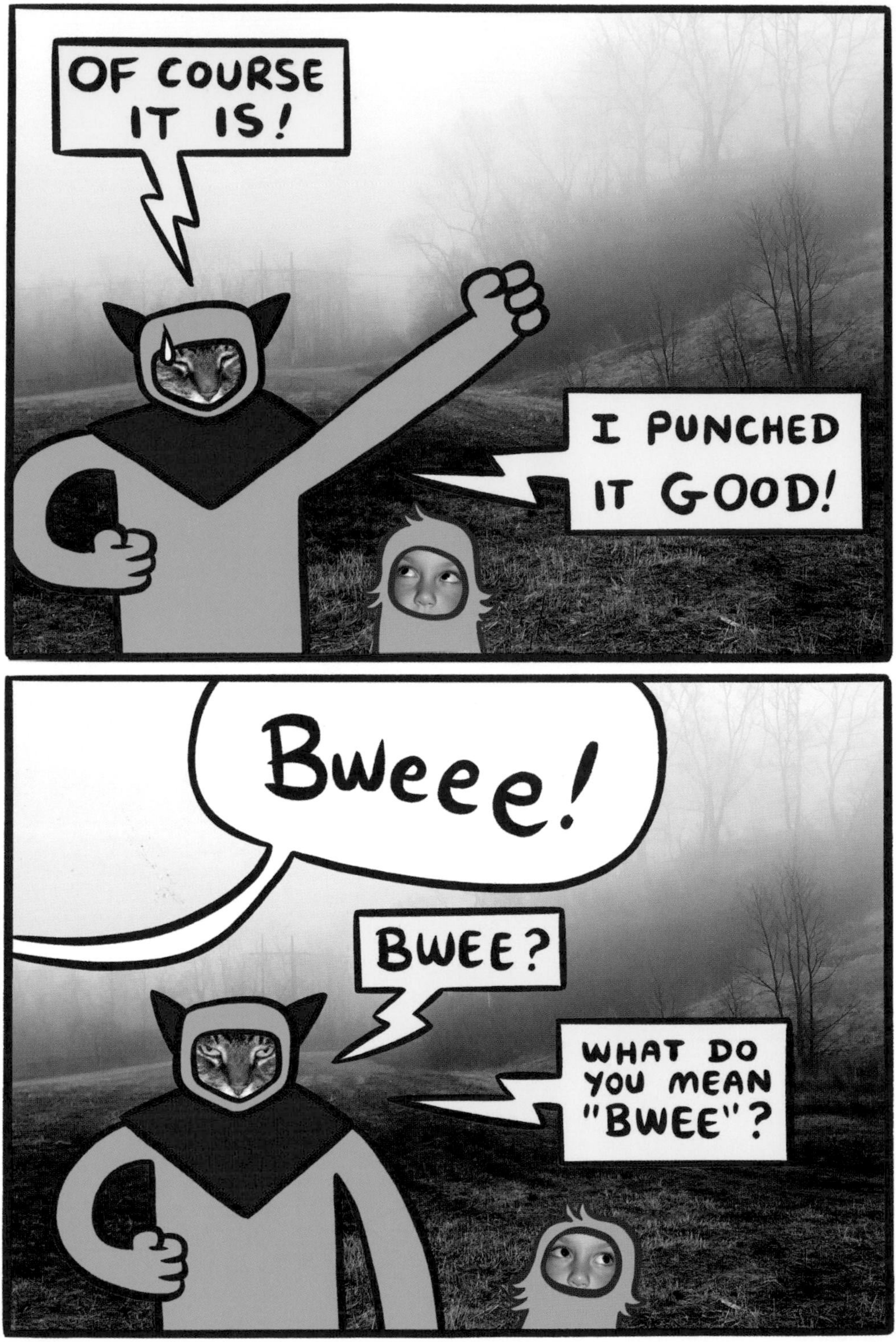
OF COURSE IT IS!
I PUNCHED IT GOOD!
Bweee!
BWEE?
WHAT DO YOU MEAN "BWEE"?

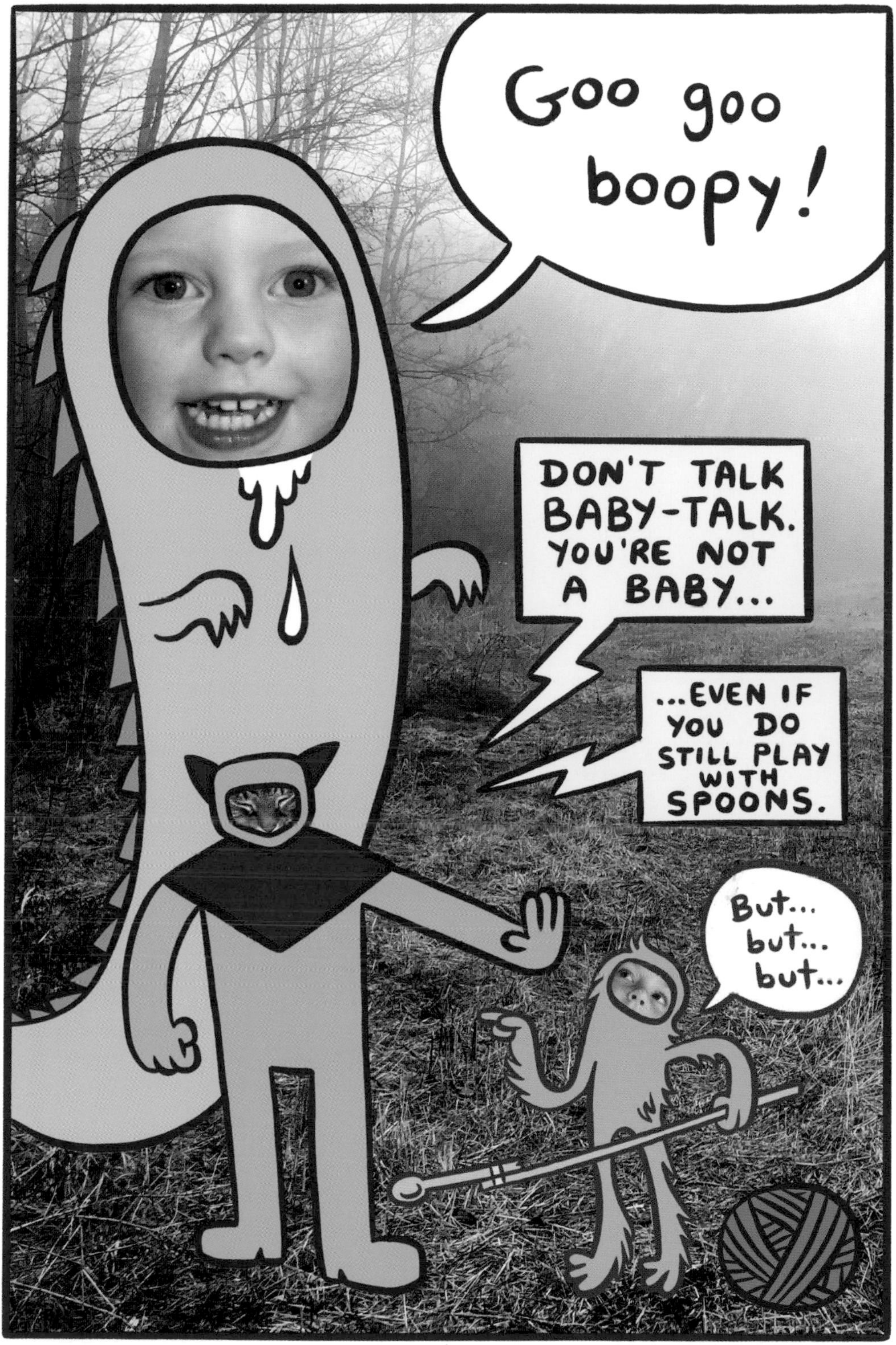
Goo goo boopy!
DON'T TALK BABY-TALK. YOU'RE NOT A BABY...
...EVEN IF YOU DO STILL PLAY WITH SPOONS.
But... but... but...

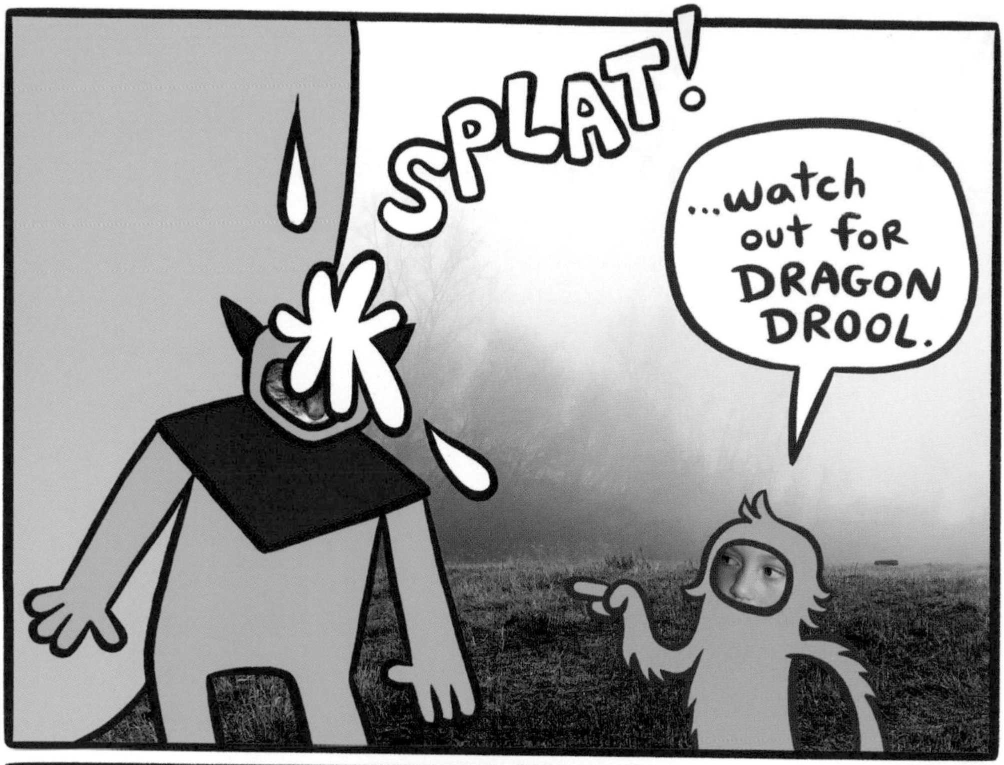
SPLAT!
...watch out for DRAGON DROOL.

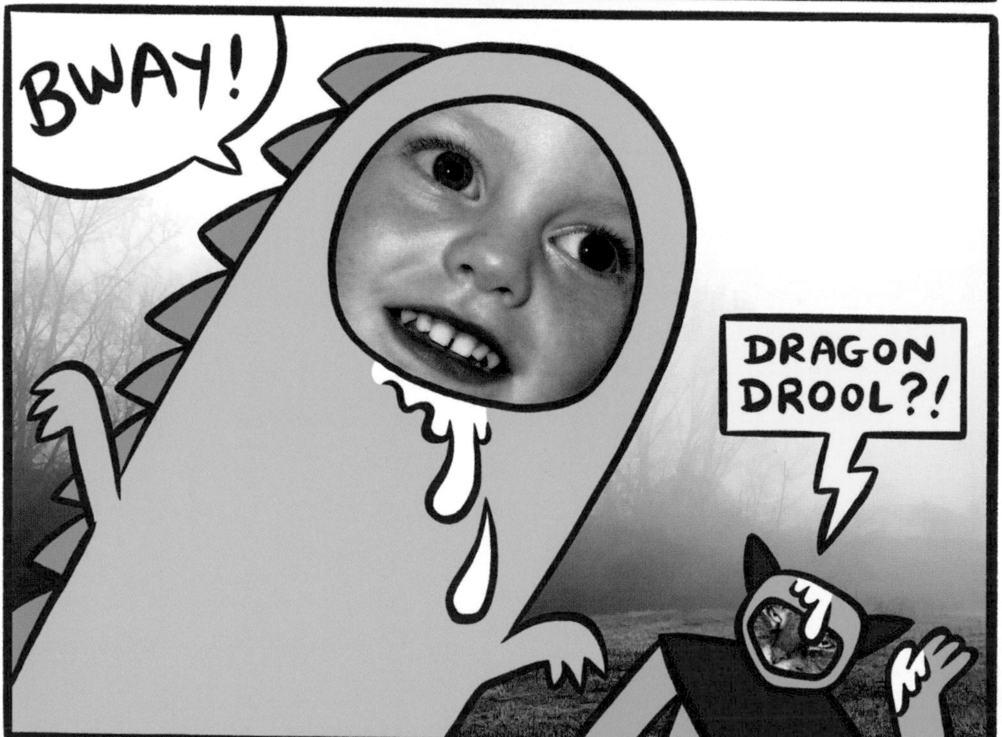
BWAY!
DRAGON DROOL?!

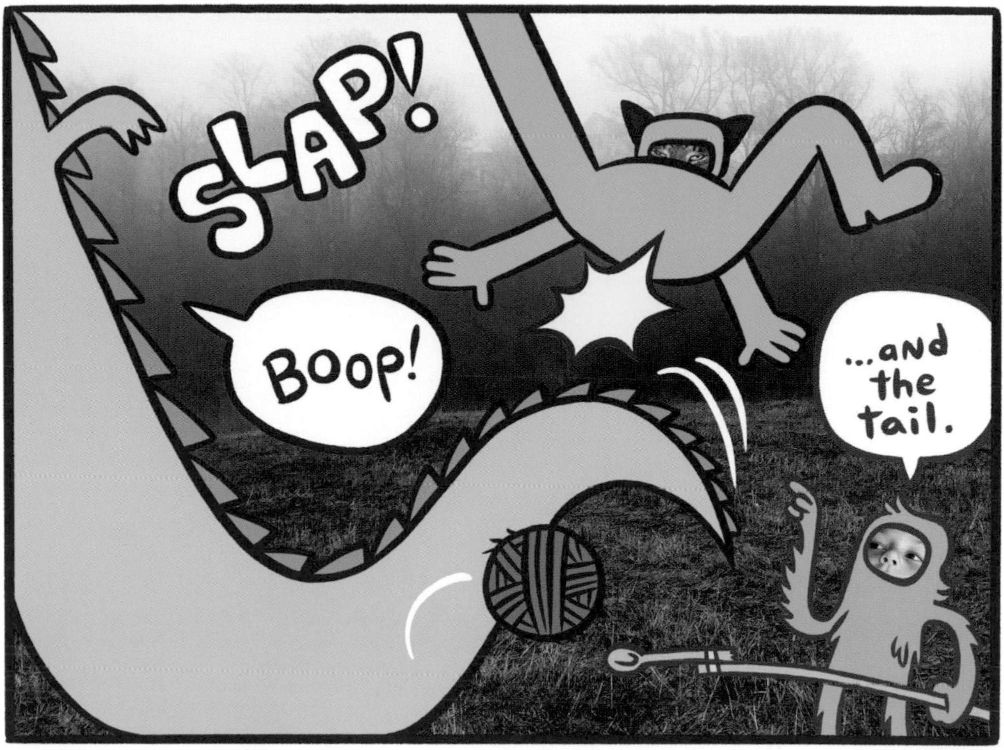
SLAP!
BOOP!
...and the tail.

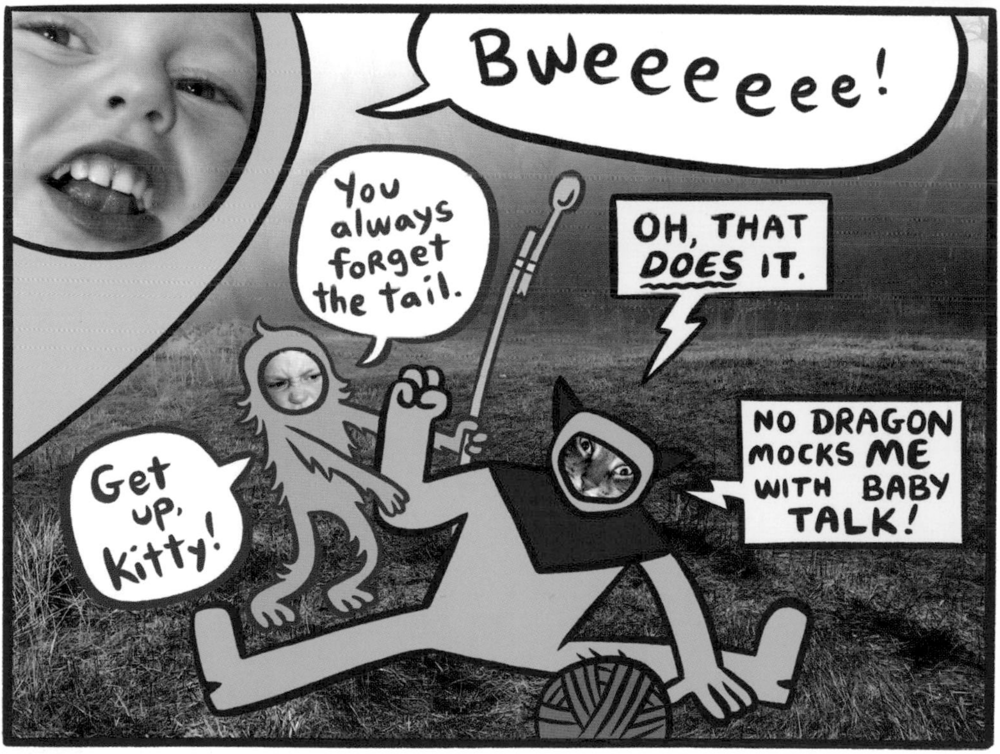
Bweeeeee!
You always forget the tail.
OH, THAT DOES IT.
NO DRAGON MOCKS ME WITH BABY TALK!
Get up, Kitty!

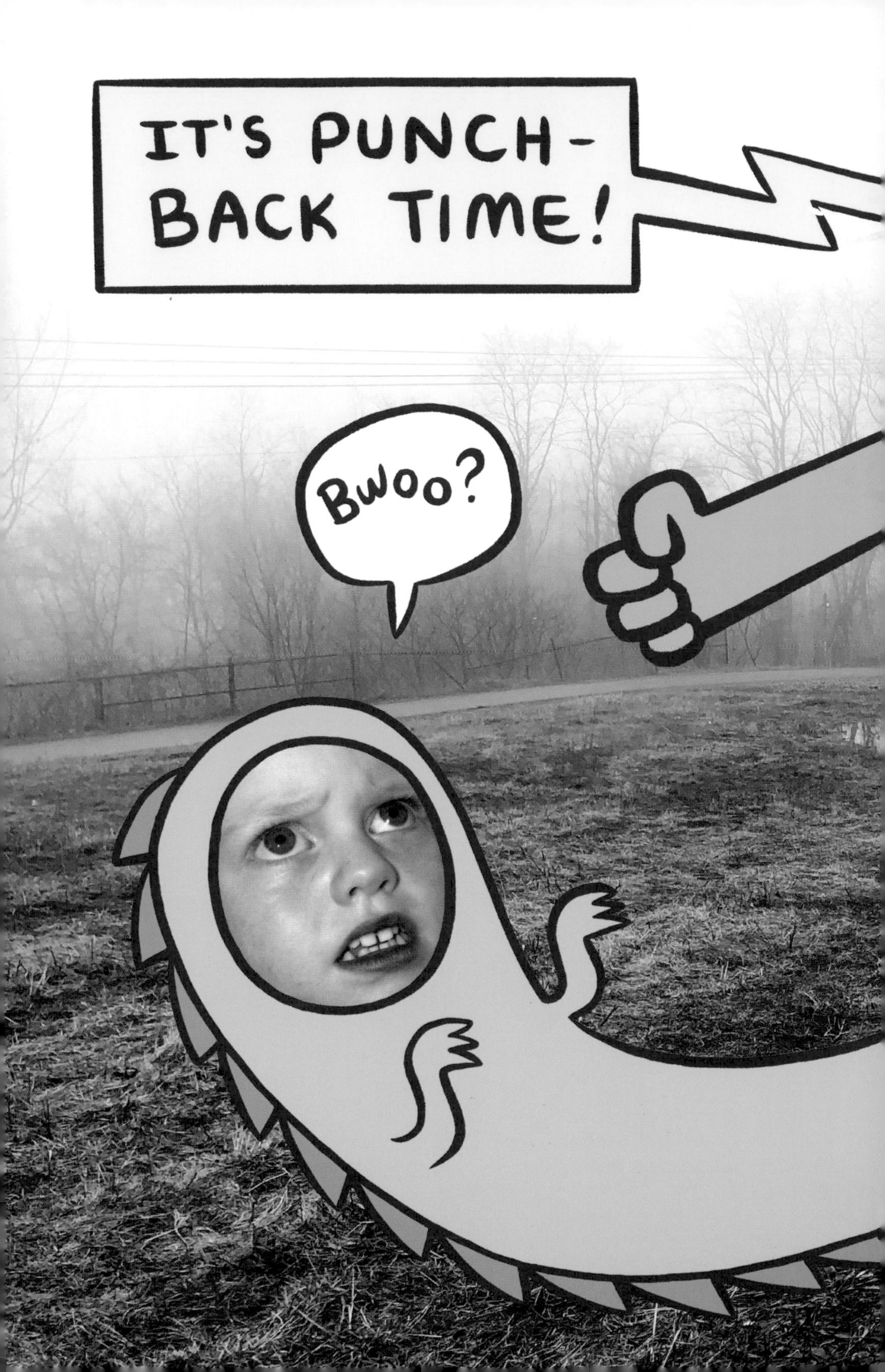
IT'S PUNCH-BACK TIME!
BWOO?

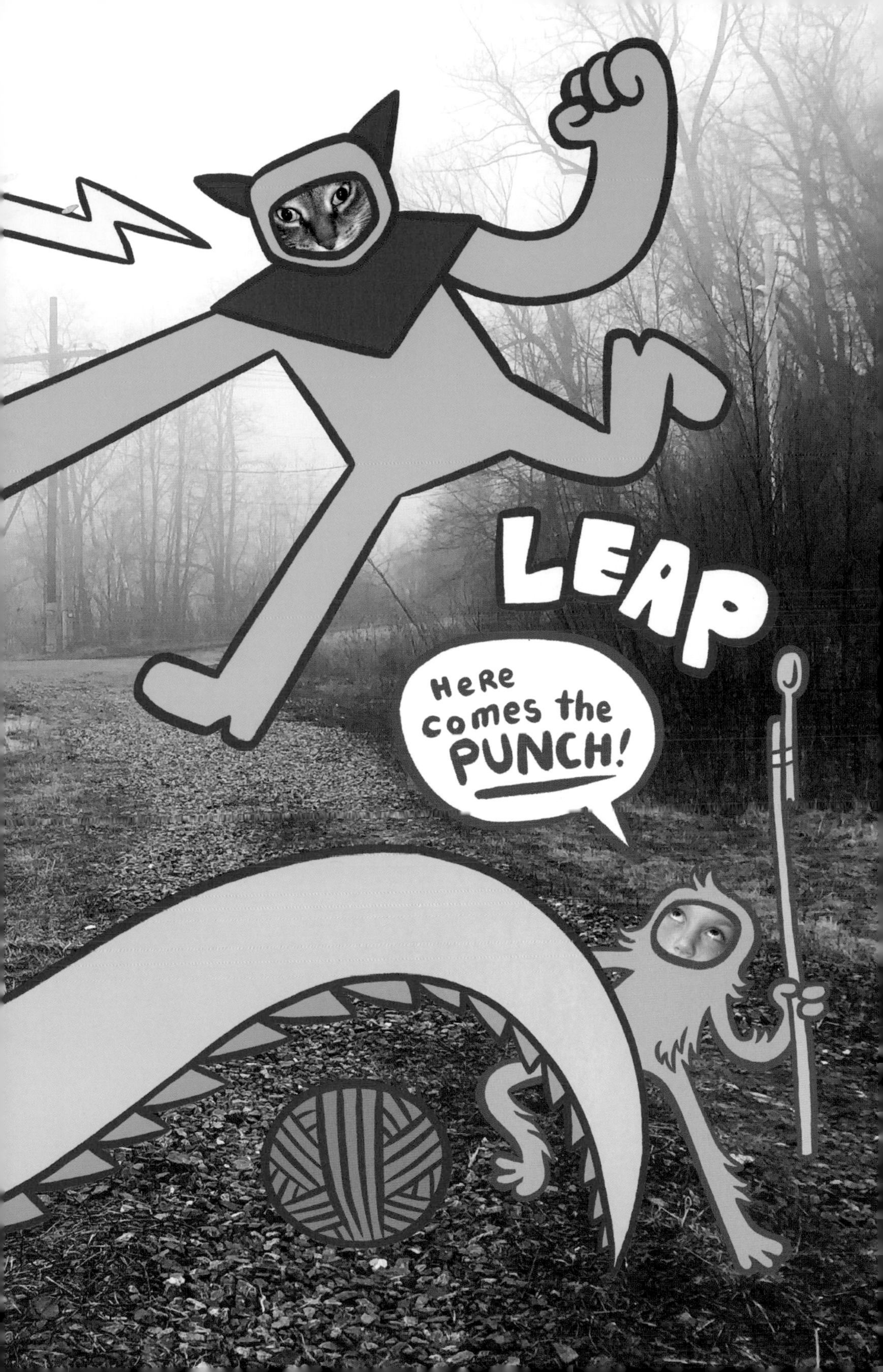
LEAP
Here comes the PUNCH!

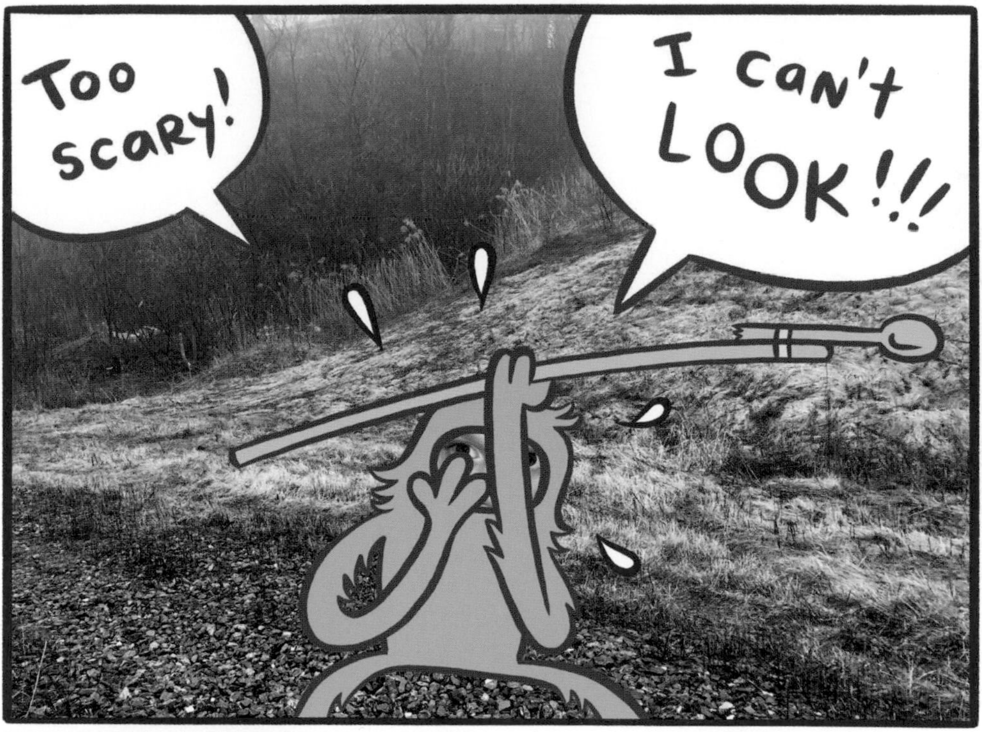
Too scary!
I can't LOOK!!!

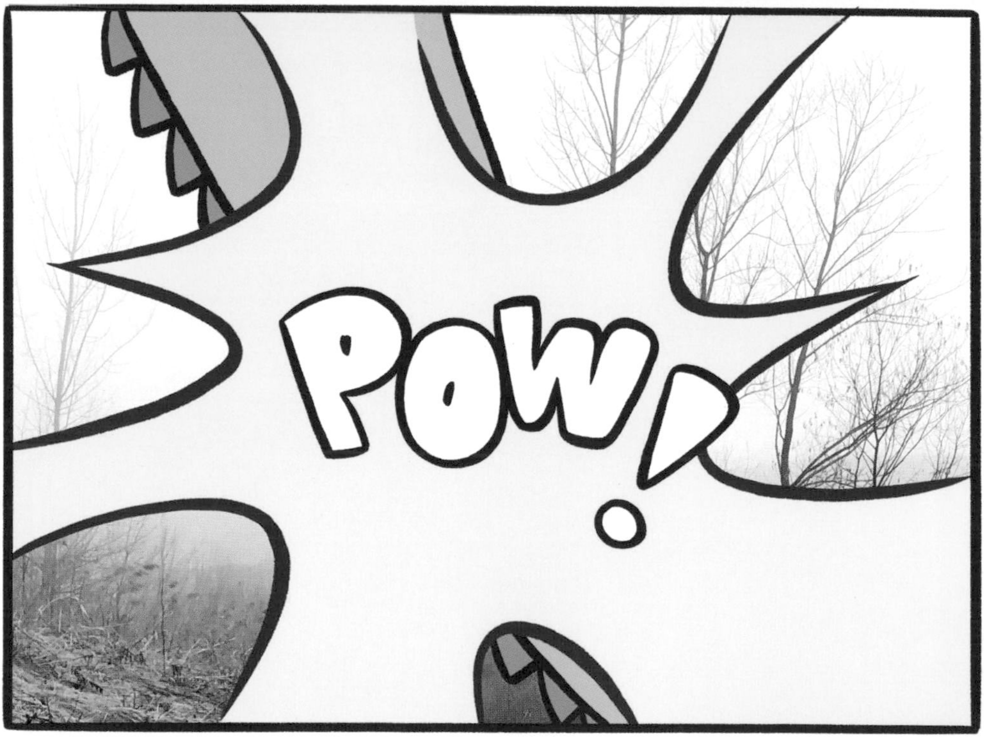
POW!

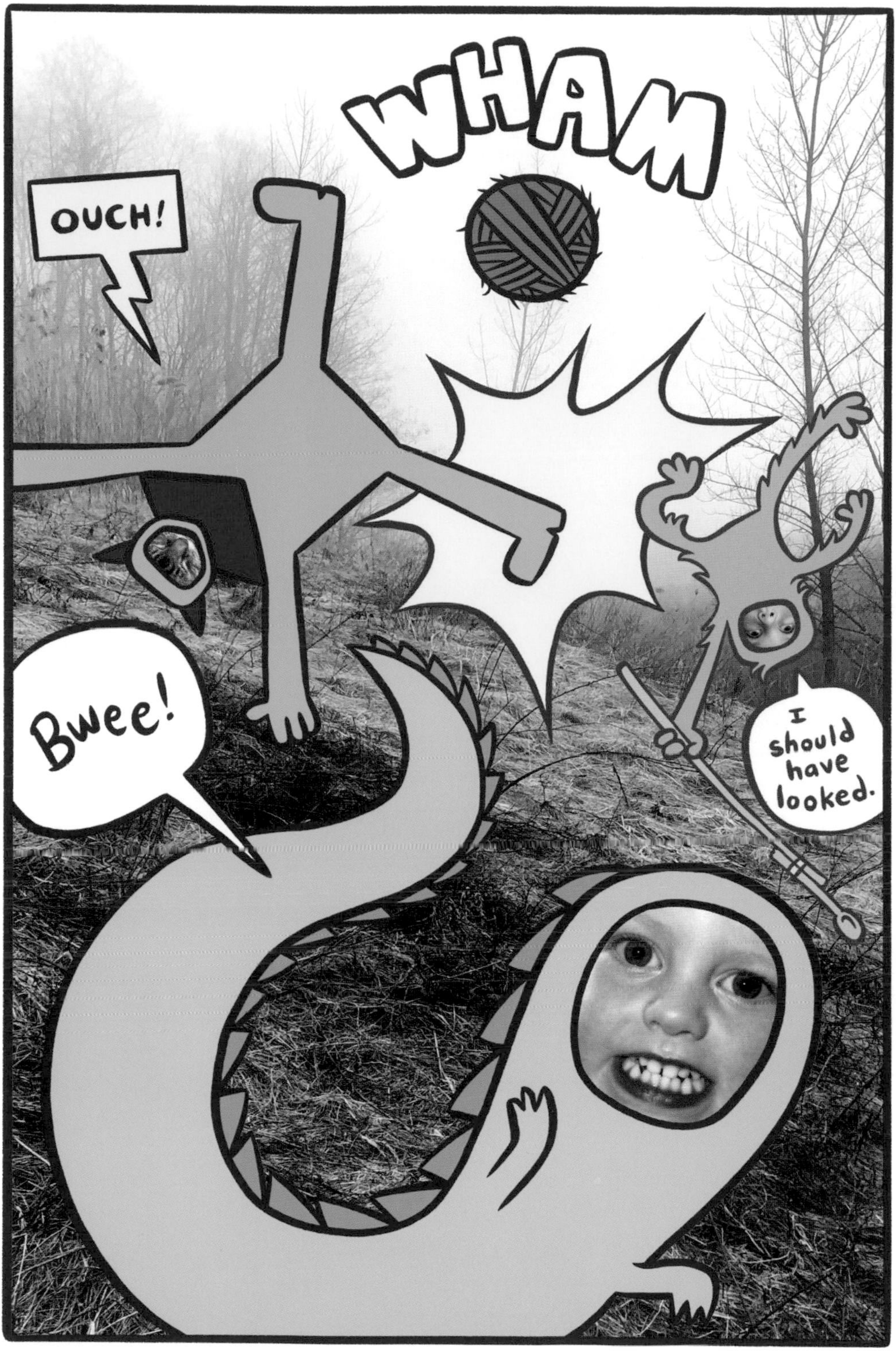
WHAM
OUCH!
Bwee!
I should have looked.

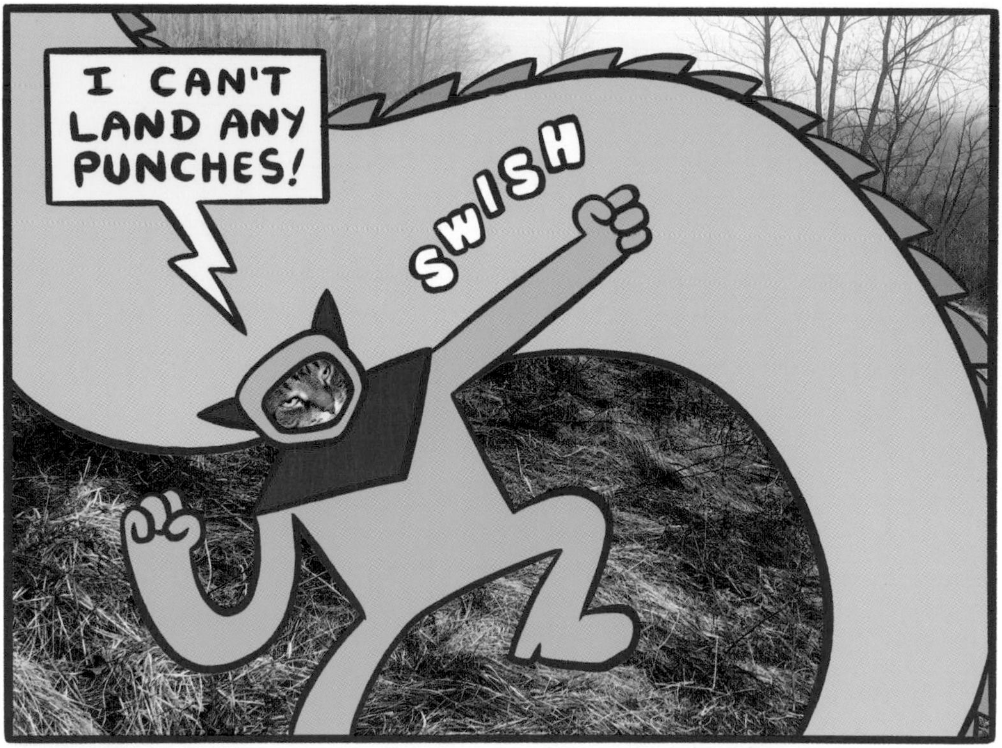
I CAN'T LAND ANY PUNCHES!
SWISH

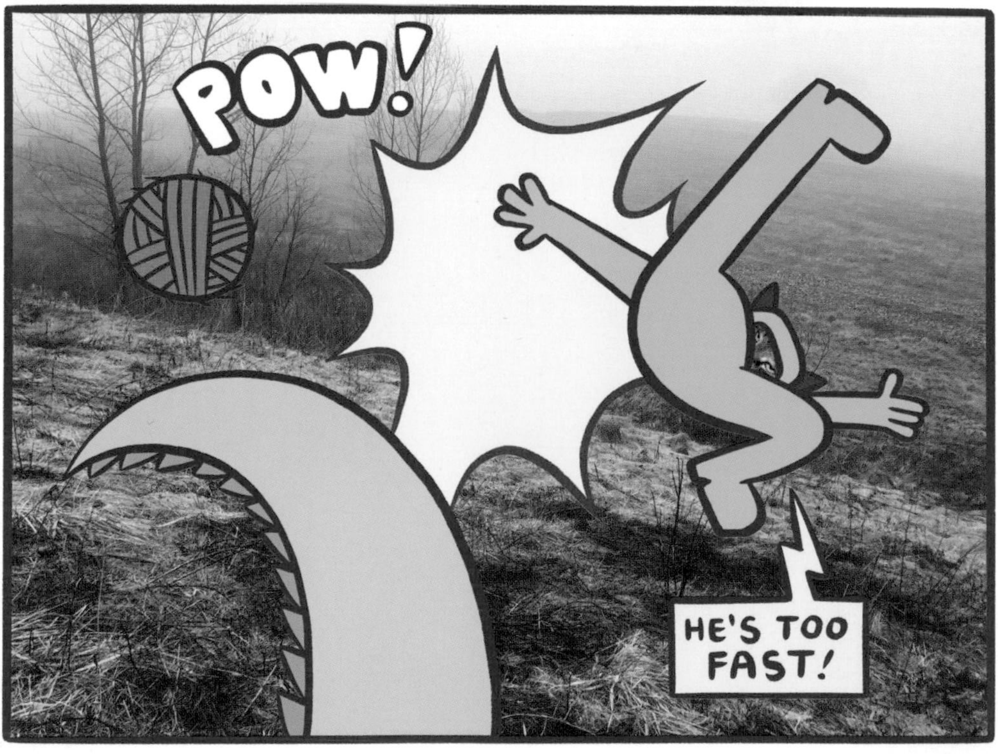
POW!
HE'S TOO FAST!

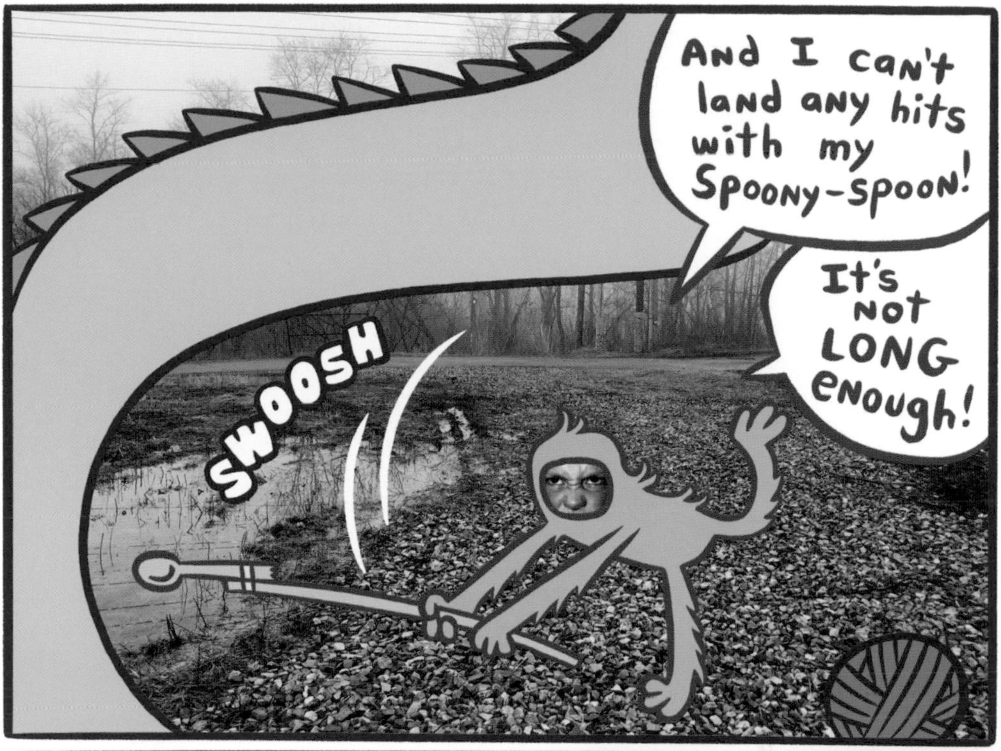
And I can't land any hits with my Spoony-spoon!
It's not LONG enough!
SWOOSH

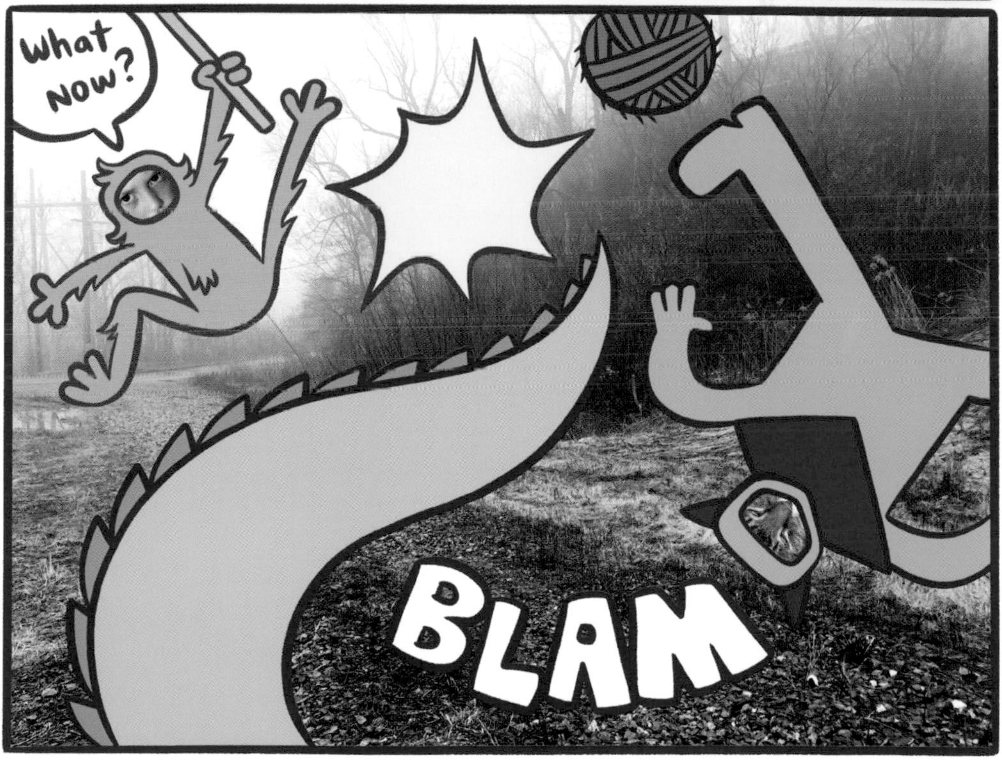
What now?
BLAM

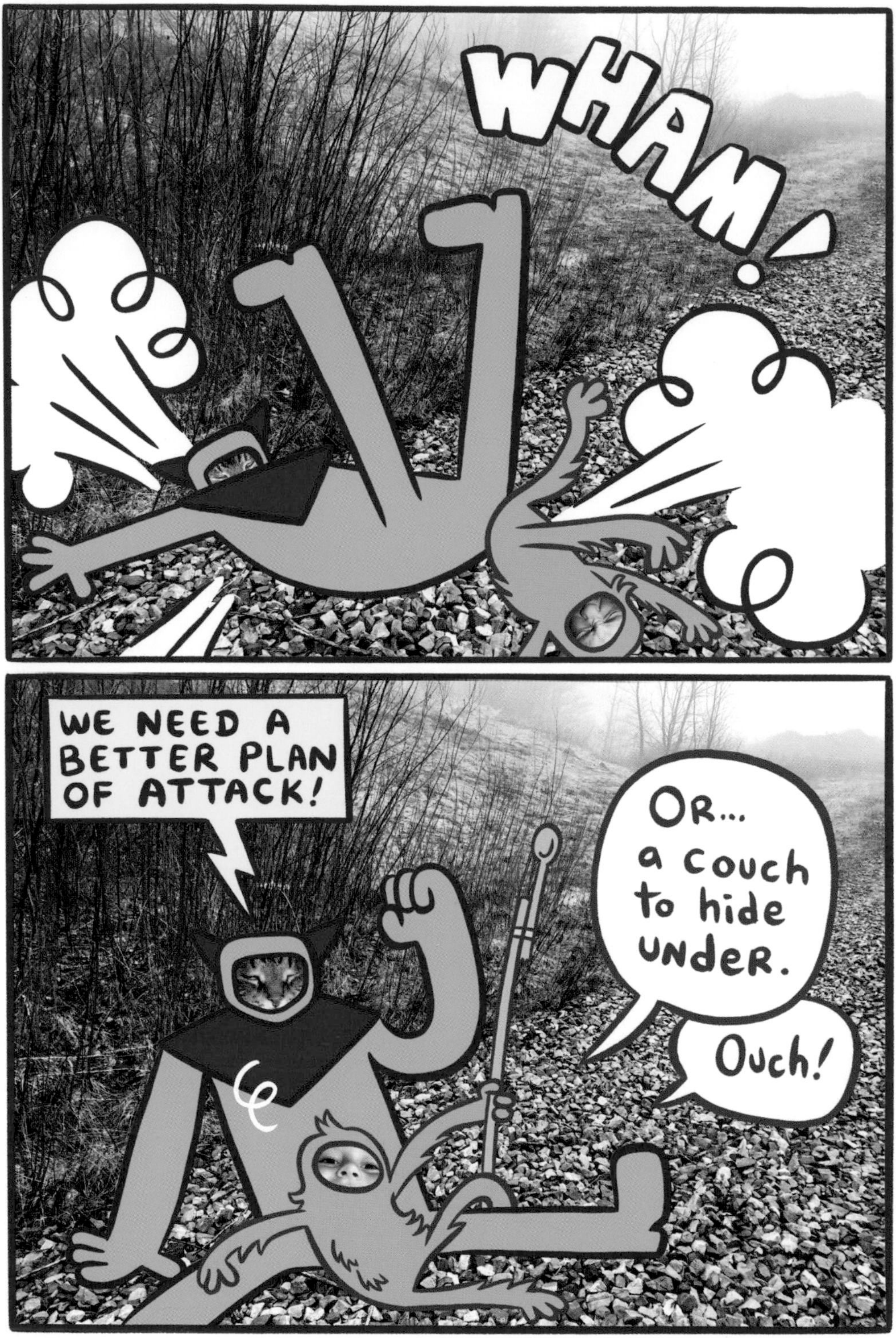
WHAM!
WE NEED A BETTER PLAN OF ATTACK!
Or... a couch to hide under.
Ouch!

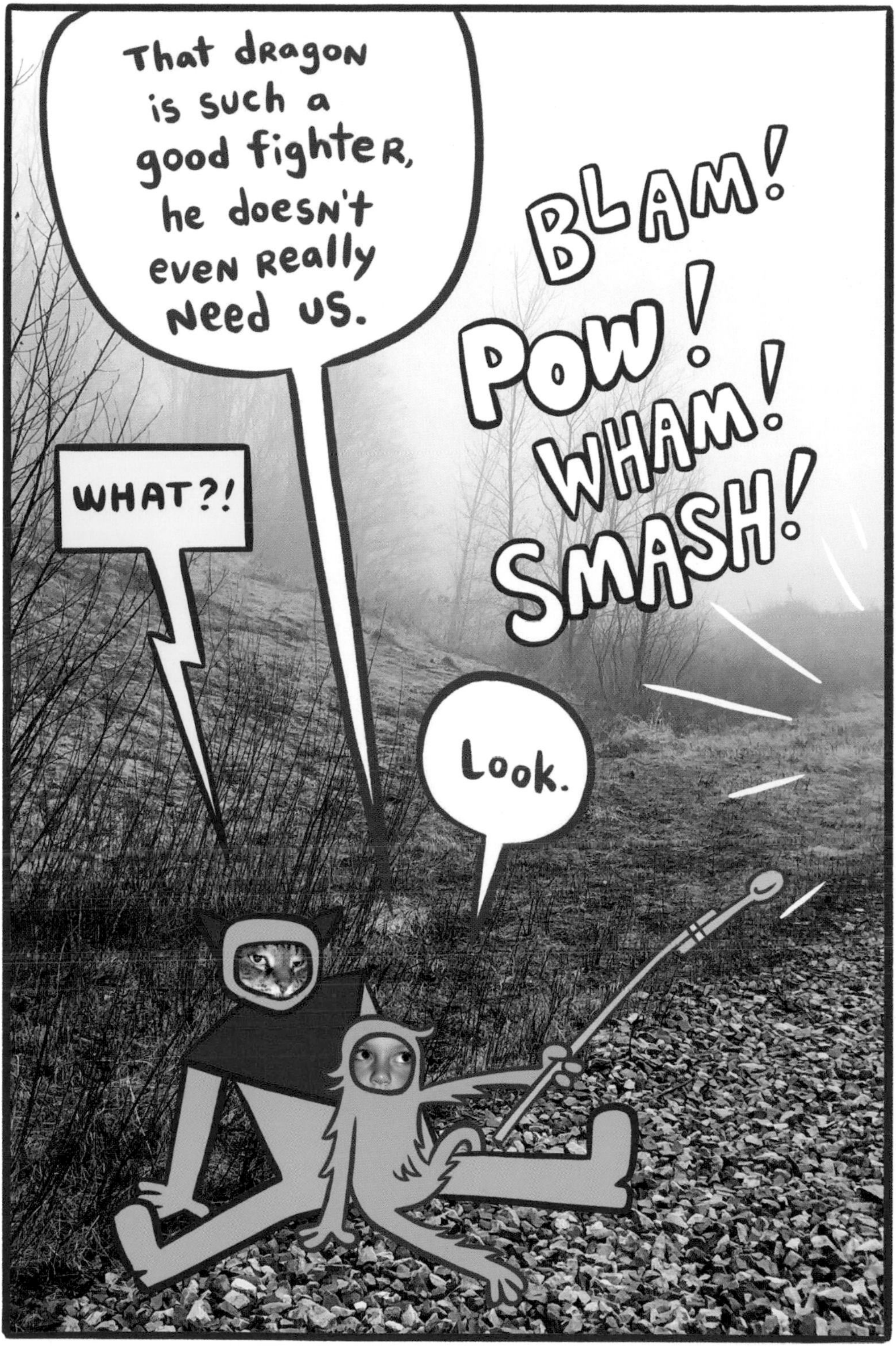
That dragon is such a good fighter, he doesn't even really need us.
BLAM!
POW!
WHAM!
SMASH!
WHAT?!
Look.

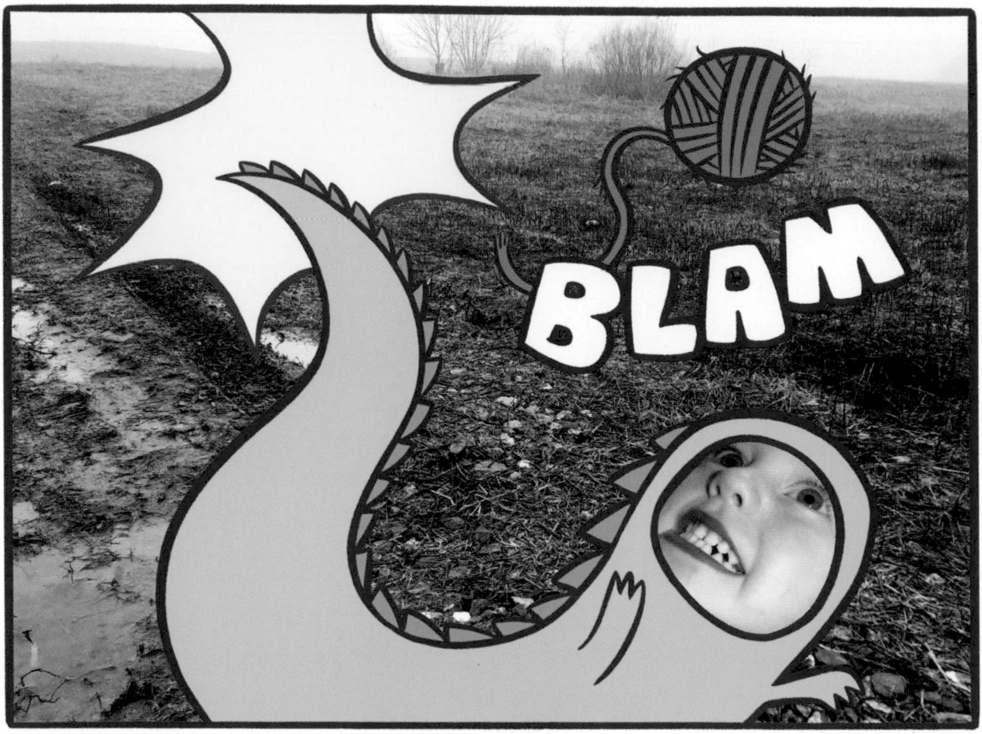
BLAM
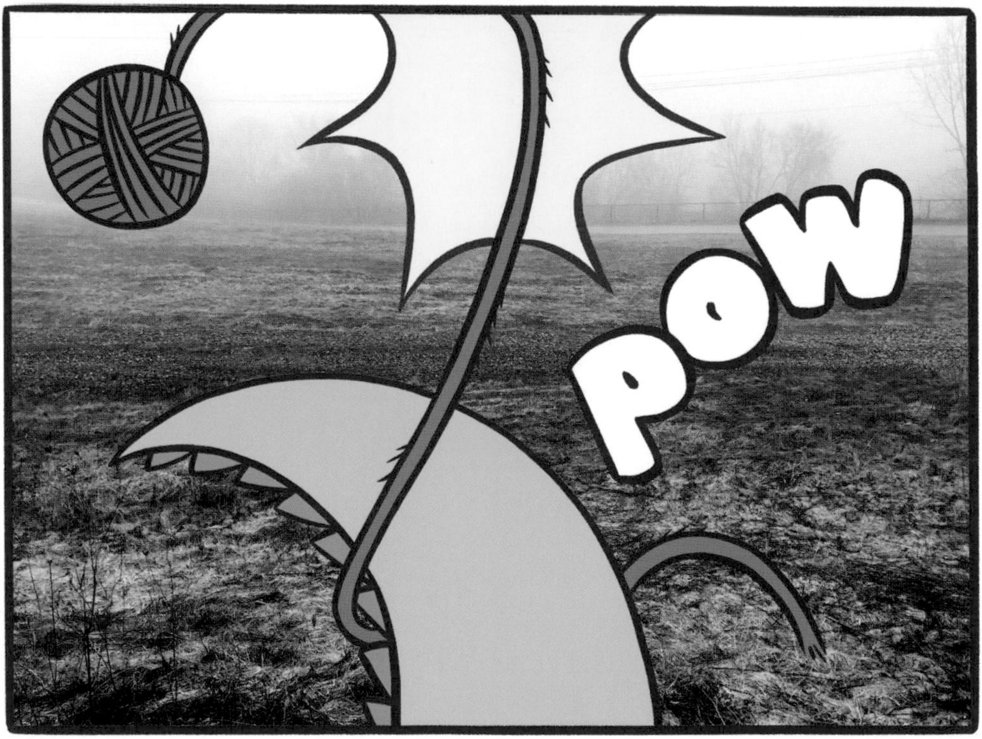
POW

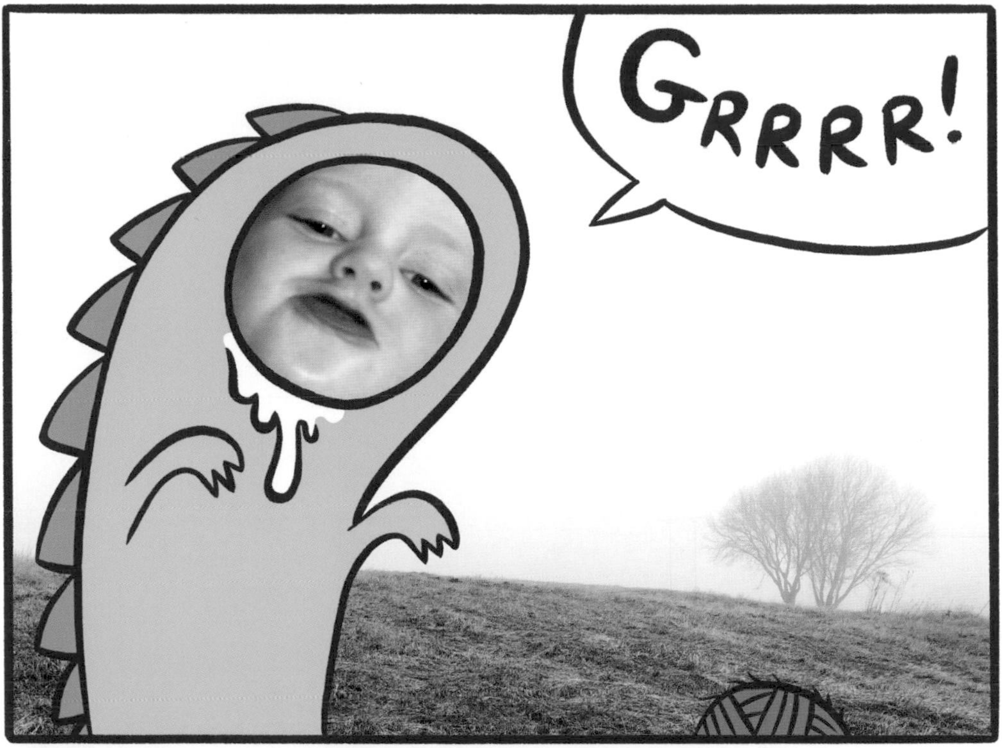
GRRRR!

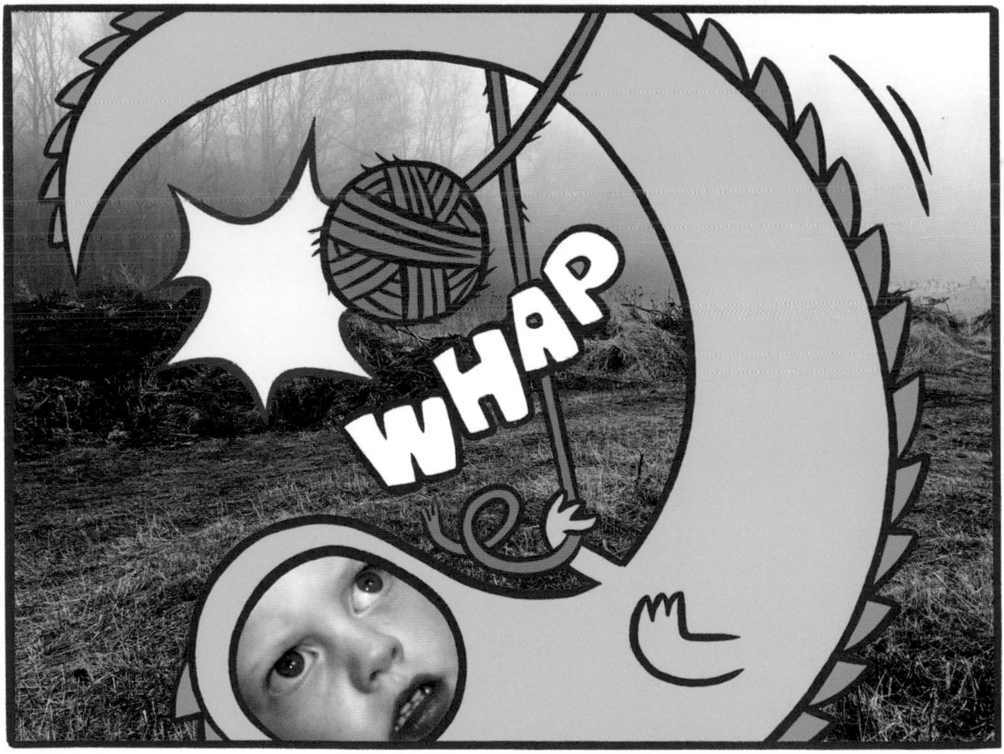
WHAP

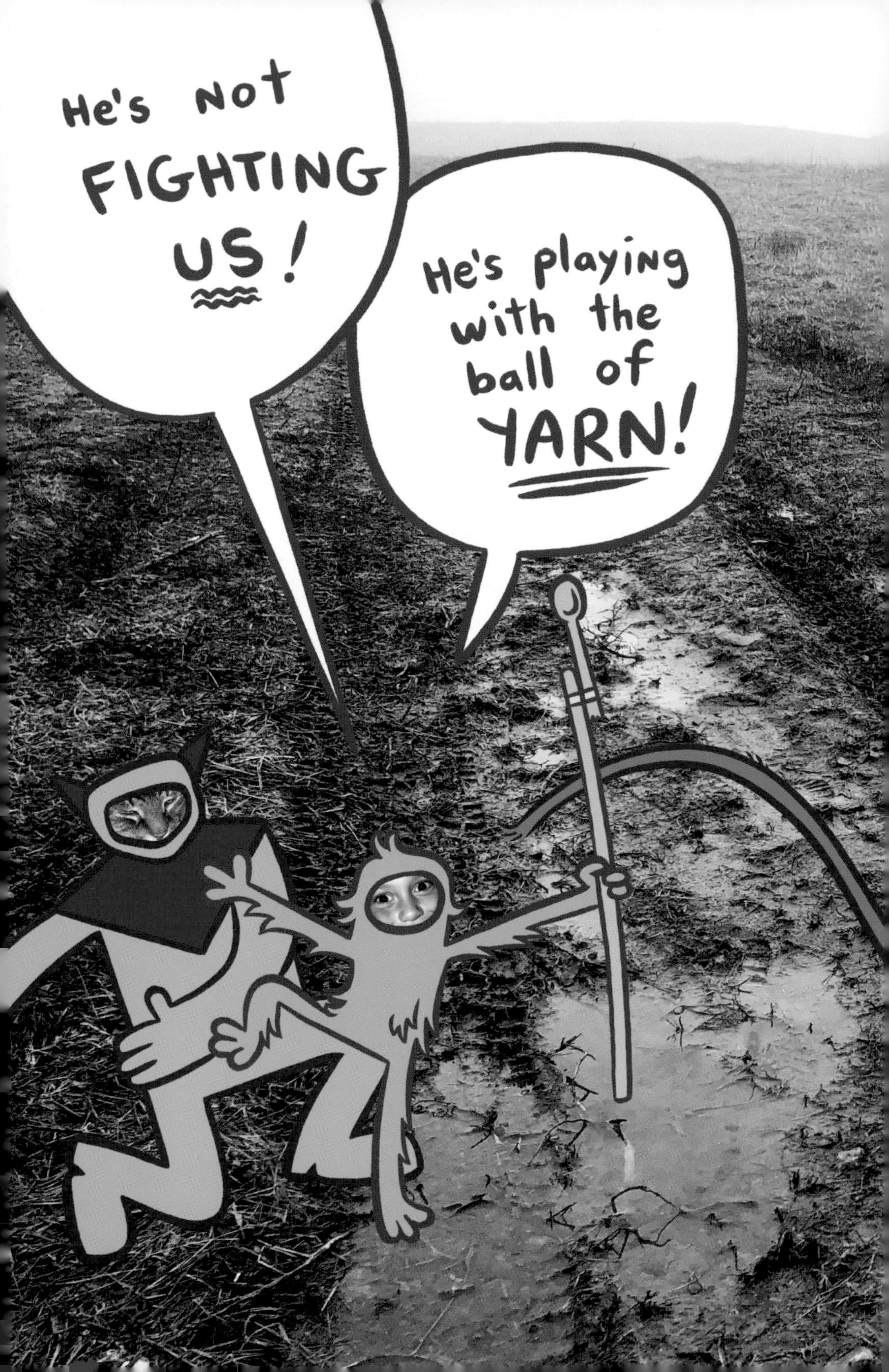
He's not FIGHTING US!
He's playing with the ball of YARN!

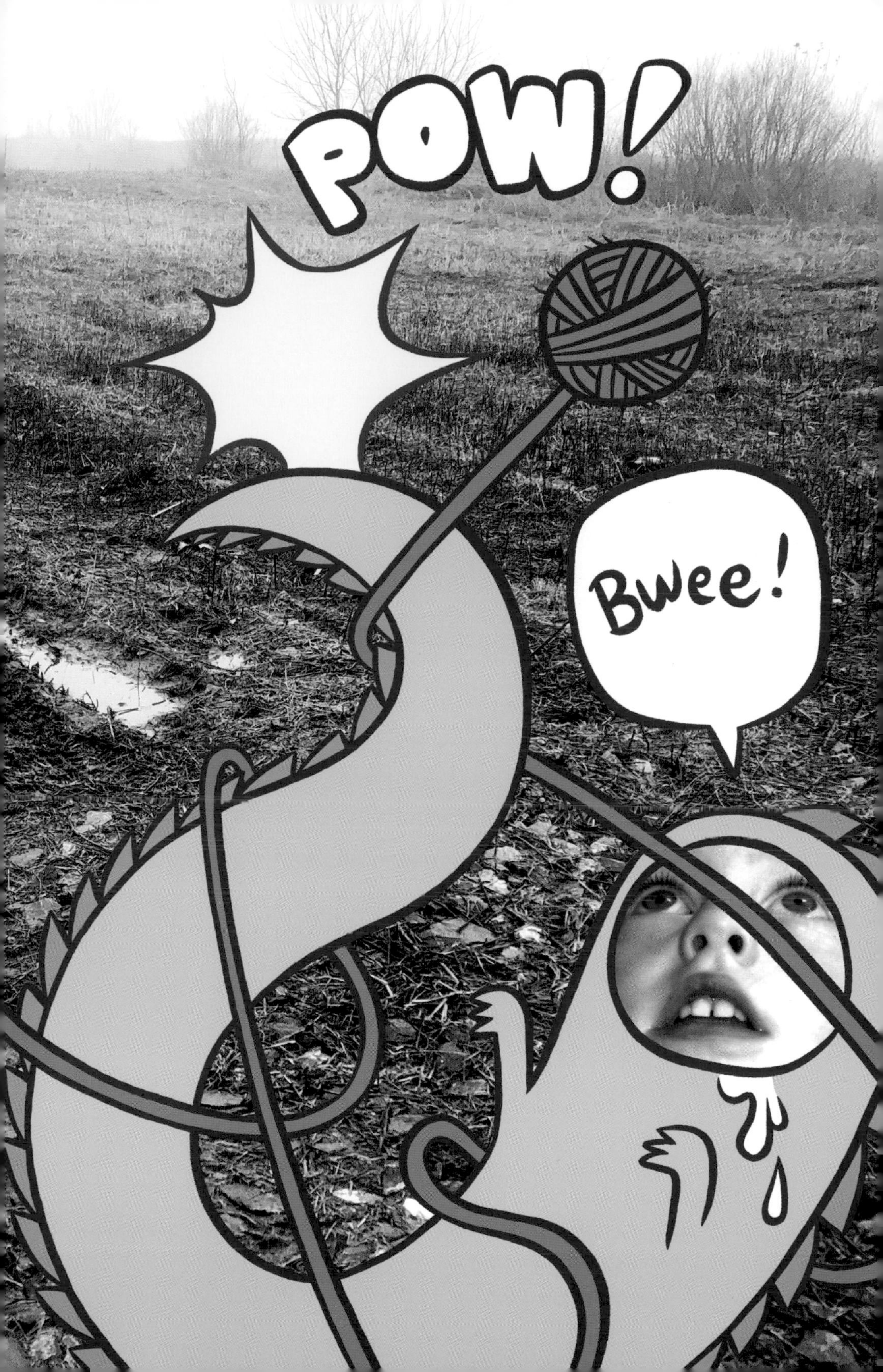
POW!
Bwee!

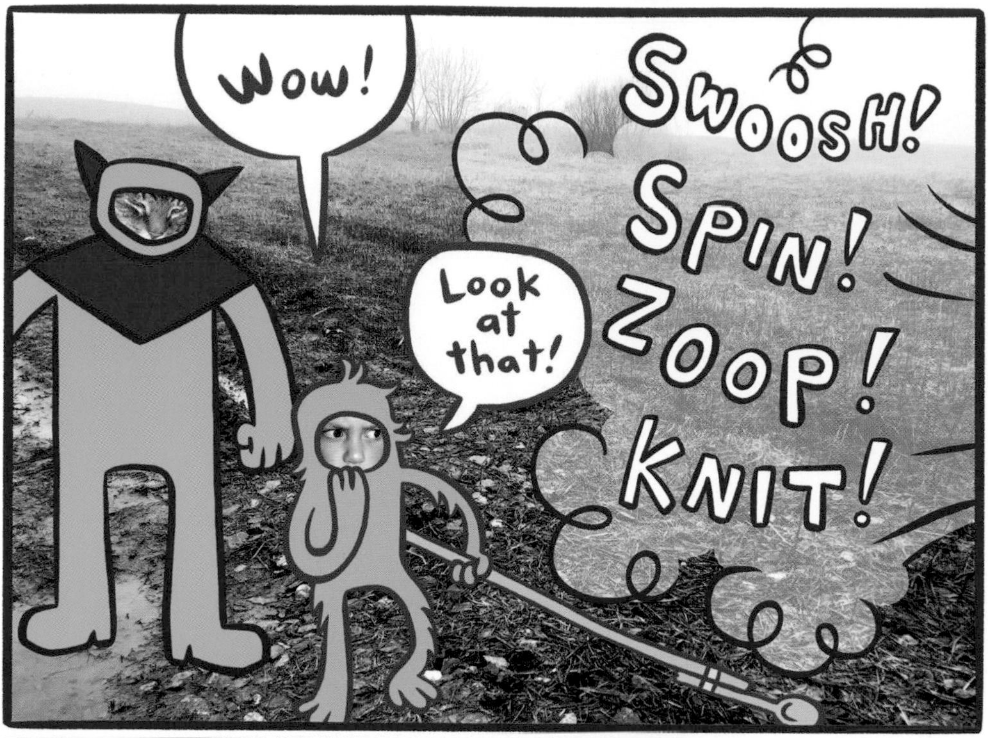
Wow!
Look at that!
SWOOSH!
SPIN!
ZOOP!
KNIT!

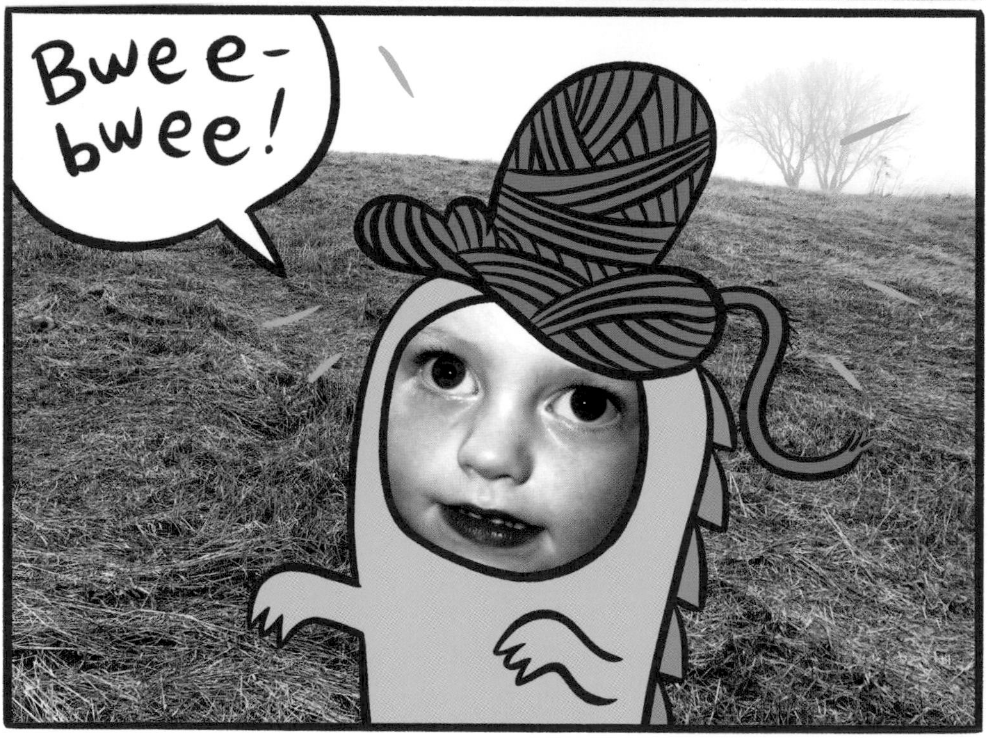
Bwee-bwee!

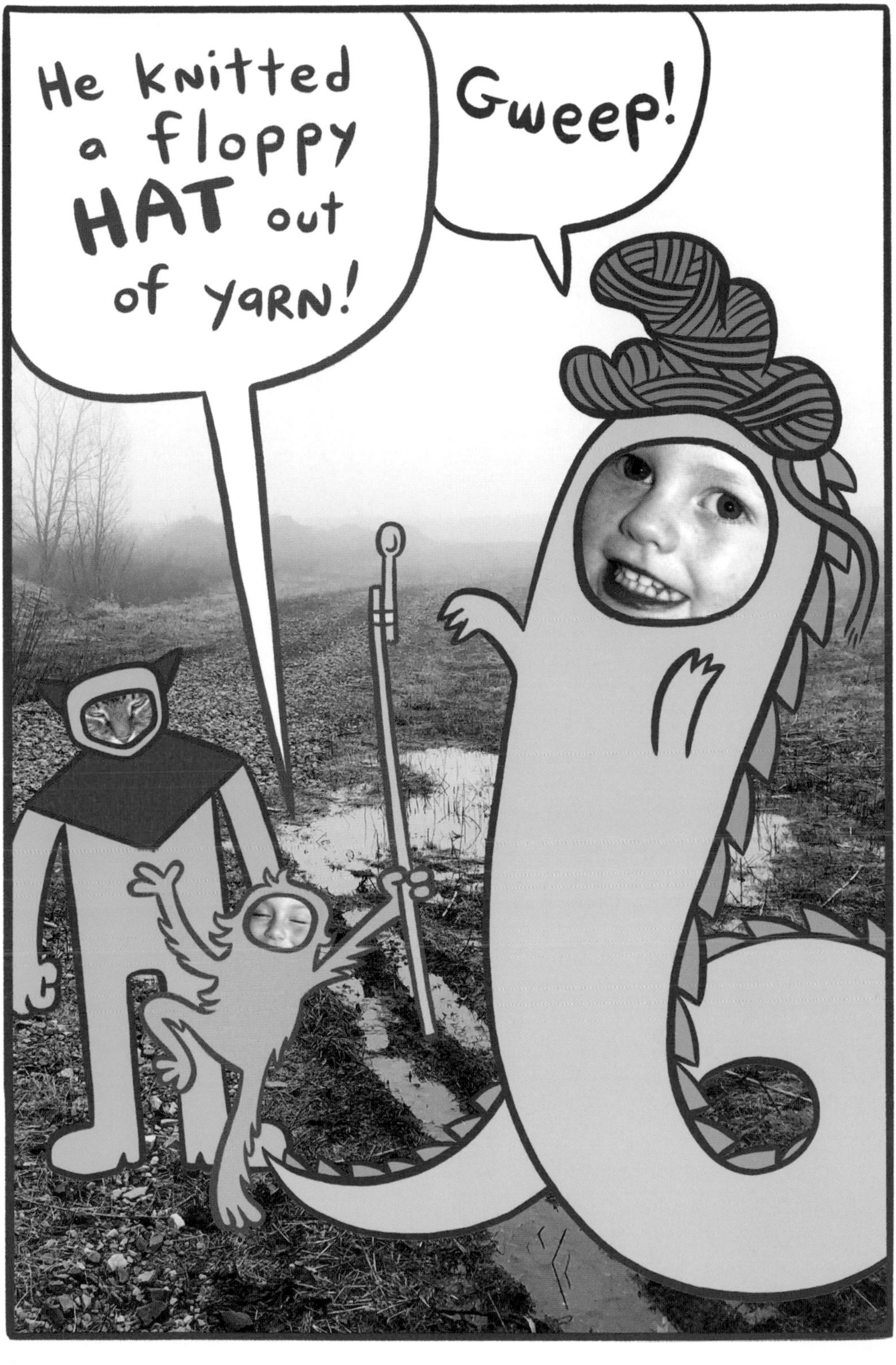
He knitted a floppy HAT out of yarn!
Gweep!

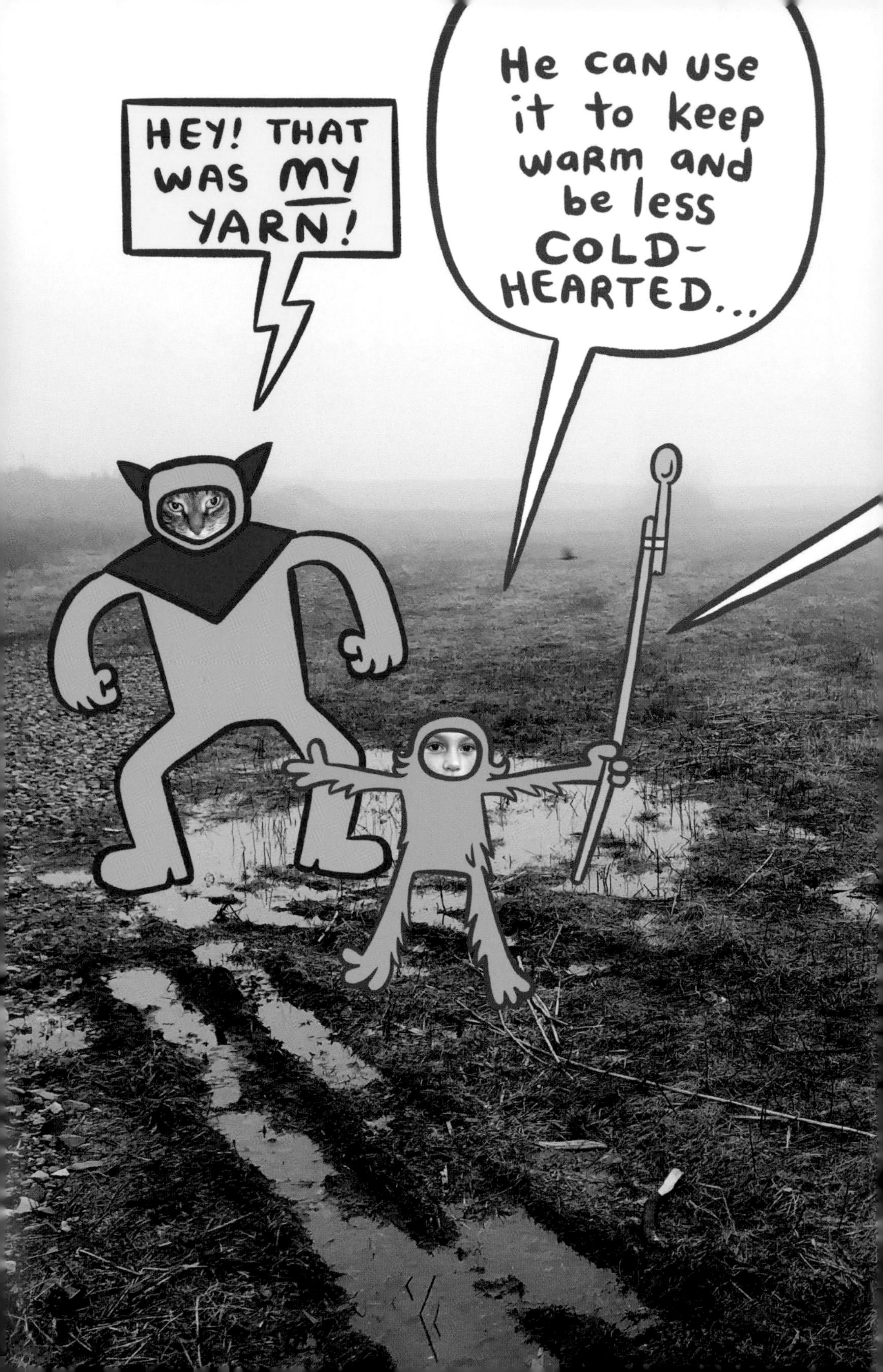
HEY! THAT WAS MY YARN!
He can use it to keep warm and be less COLD-HEARTED...

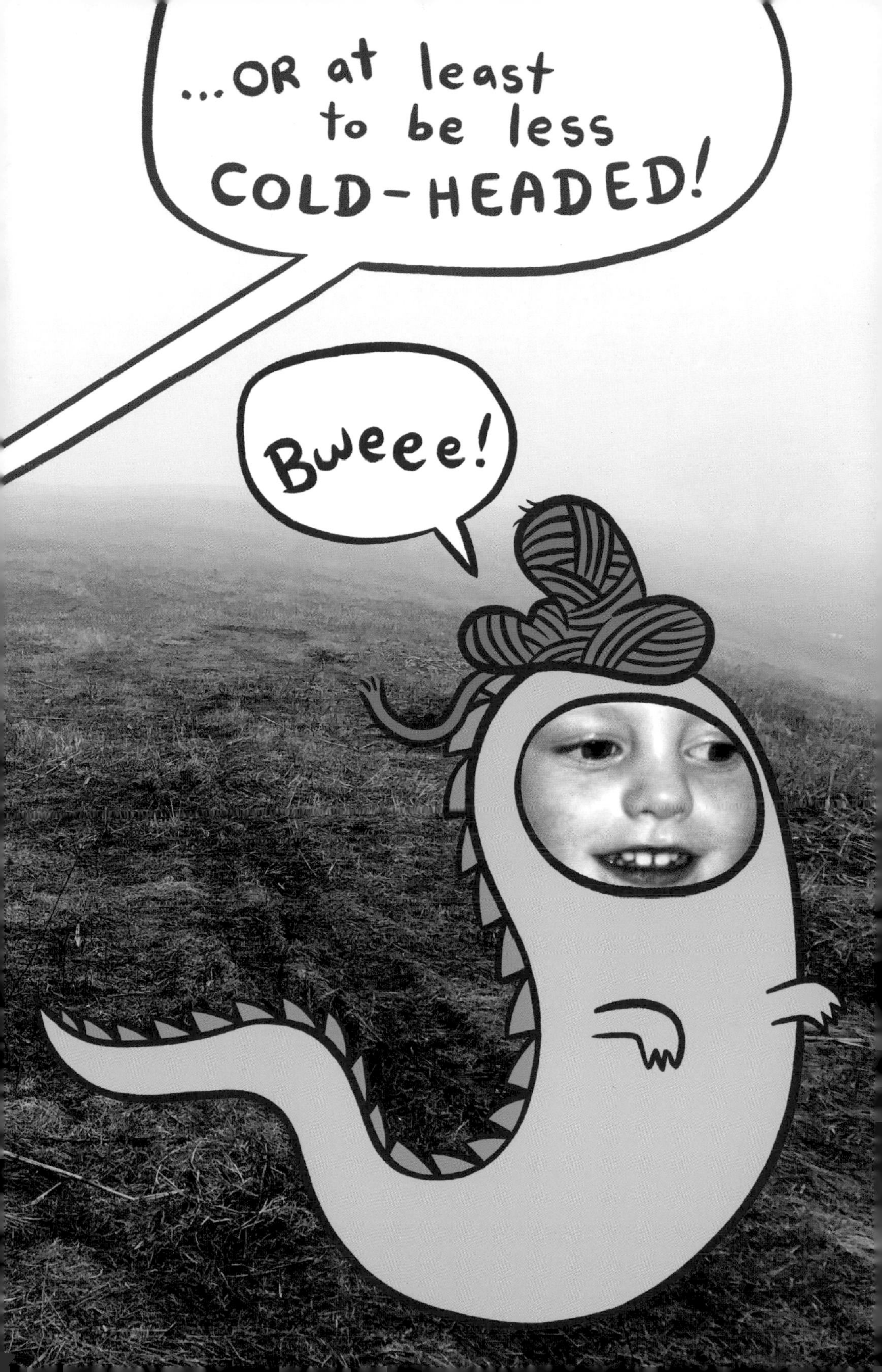
...OR at least to be less COLD-HEADED!
Bweee!

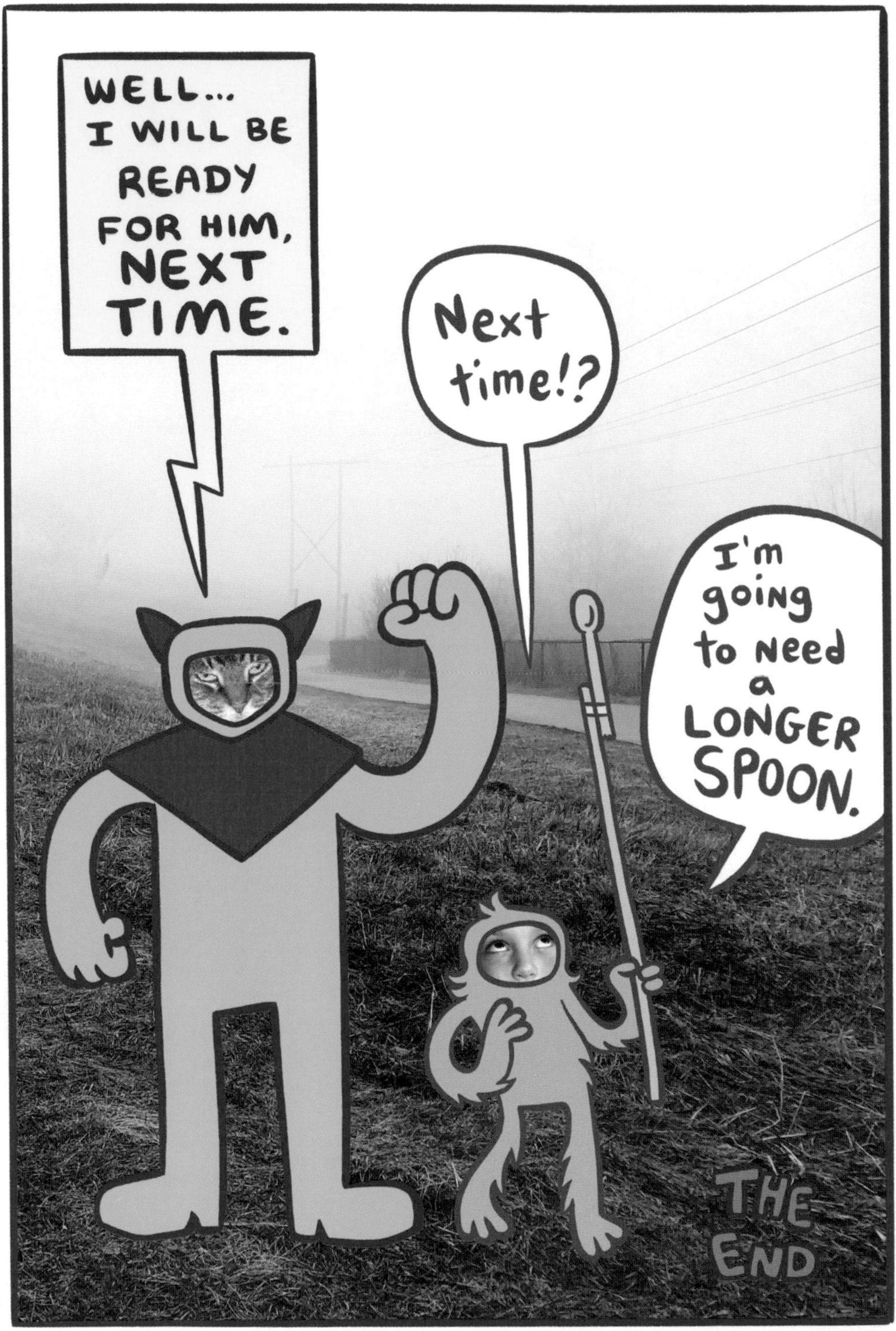
WELL...
I WILL BE
READY
FOR HIM,
NEXT
TIME.
Next
time!?
I'm
going
to need
a
LONGER
SPOON.
THE
END